fubar

SIN CITY MC - OAKLAND CHAPTER

MICHEL PRINCE

one

THERE WAS a thin line between intelligence and insanity. The idea that someone was too smart for their own good wasn't an allegory, it was a warning. For Daniel "Fubar" Coney, he tended to teeter a bit to the crazy. He wasn't stupid by any stretch of the imagination. *Hyper stimulated* is what they'd said when they suggested to ply him with drugs to tamp down the bells and whistles distracting him in class. What they never considered was the fact he was overstimulated because the questions, lectures, or activities bored him. Not because he didn't like the subject, he just didn't need the repetition to keep the information in his brain others tended to need. One and done, like most of the women he fucked. Been there, done that, got the T-shirt, and saw no reason for a second ride.

The Sin City MC he belonged to was going to call him Twitch, until the Prez, Grimm, saw him fighting with his father in the parking lot when he was just a Prospect, the hero cop Sean Coney telling him he was fucking up his life and it wouldn't be tolerated. Choices had to be made, and without a second thought, Fubar had tossed his house key to his father and walked into the strip club as his dad called out, "You want to be a fuckup, be a fuckup! Just don't ask me to use a hook to get you out of jail. Stay here and you'll be locked up within a year."

"You think that's a challenge to make it three hundred and sixty-six days?" Fubar said as he walked up to Ice at the bar and lifted a finger to get a beer brought over.

"Careful there," Maxwell "Ice" Winter, the man who'd brought him into the MC, said. "He could get you on underage drinking."

"He would too," Fubar responded. "As if he didn't pass me a shot of Jack when I was twelve saying some shit about becoming a man."

"Did he bring you to the Bunny Ranch too?" Ice laughed.

"Not until I was thirteen. I think he was trying to get me to go to sleep with the whiskey. Guess it worked when I was teething," he said before taking a swallow from the bottle set before him. "Bunny Ranch was for him, though, couldn't go in the back. They just babysat me while he inspected—"

Reality smacked him in the face because he hadn't ever revisited the memory of when he went out to the legal brothel in the county proper.

"That motherfucker, he was cheating on my mama."

Ice narrowed his eyes at him. "How many times were you dropped on your head as a child?"

. . .

No reason to explain he was a savant in many ways, but had tended to be slow on some uptakes. Social cues were something he had to learn the hard way. Shit, for years he didn't get that women were practically throwing themselves at him, until a bold one said directly she wanted to fuck him. He'd gotten better since joining the MC, hard not to with people pointing out the obvious to most with a "normal" brain. If nothing else, the man was a quick study.

From that moment on, he'd been Fubar, *fucked up beyond all recognition*. He let them think he was simple and slow with only the id part of his brain functioning. In some ways he had to admit he was very much driven by the primate part of himself, running into situations most would run away from. He had a survival instinct. Sadly he'd inherited the hero gene from his father and always wanted to make sure he rescued anyone in danger first. Here his dad was worried he'd be a firefighter. Now the man would love to have him riding on the back of a red truck working for the city instead of straddling a Black Denim Harley Breakout 117 running drugs for the Sin City MC.

For Fubar, triggers had always been strange things, as if every time one was pulled, you were shooting out of a starting block. Running, swimming, a bell goes off, and your horse bolts from the gate. In many ways he was trained to respond, run fast, turn left, and go until he exhausted himself. He learned early in life, when you hear bullets, run. Only he ran toward and not away. He'd blame it on being dyslexic, but that was probably the only psych diagnosis he hadn't tested positive for.

There was a blanking out he disappeared into when he became the hero no one asked for. It was this void he was currently in, and he knew he should find a way to get out of the tunnel and back to the real world. Most times it was Ice's voice yanking him out of the oblivion. Maybe they should have called him Fido or Rex. He was basically a trained attack dog. Only problem, Ice was currently hitting Disneyland with the family.

"Promise me you'll stay out of trouble while I'm in Cali," Ice warned as he was packing up his twins and Bree was loading up a cooler.

"Me? What trouble could I possibly get in without you for two days?" Fubar jested.

"Five, I'll be gone for five days," Ice said, his hardened features a warning as if he wasn't sure he could leave a teenager alone with a Black Card and an unlocked liquor cabinet.

"Oh, well in that case, all fire, flood, and general body damage is on you because we both know I can only control myself for seventy-two hours unsupervised."

"That's it. Bree, we can't—" Ice began, only to get the patented stare only an Ol' Lady with vetoing privileges around family shit could muster.

Dark eyes glared in a way both men caught a shiver as the normally cool and composed woman pointed one finger, and even Fubar knew a tick system had been implemented. The woman had taken to the MC life, but she still wanted an as-normal-as-possible childhood for Ice's twins. They'd already seen their mother murdered, and Bree was all about regular white-picket-fence-type experiences.

"Your babies have earned the highest marks in all of the first grade at school. You are taking them to Disney and will pose with princesses and action heroes."

"Wait, there'll be princesses?" Fubar teased, knowing at least

Jane, Ice's girl twin, was excited to see that. "You didn't say there would be princesses. Now I have to go."

"No, Uncle Fubar," Jane whined. "If you're there, they won't talk to me."

"Oh heck to the no," Bree said, augmenting her language as if Jane and Aiden hadn't heard worse from the men of the club. "I'm pretty sure there is an order of protection to keep you at least a hundred miles from them."

"I think they forgot to renew it," he joked. "Please, how much trouble could I possibly get into in less than a week?"

"Nope, not taking the bait," Ice said, tossing the last of the luggage into the bed of his pickup. "You'd see it as a challenge."

The challenge had not only been met, but Fubar had far exceeded even his own fucked-up record. At least he was pretty sure he had once Grimm's voice broke through his fog.

"Fucking A, Fubar, heel," Grimm's gruff voice barked at him. "Shit, shit, shit."

"Yeah, that's not coming out with a stain treater," Caliber said. As if the man had ever actually washed his own clothes.

Both men were larger than Fubar, but neither had tried to pull him off the man he'd apparently killed. Sitting back on his heels, he poked at the man's lifeless body a few times and saw the thick silver rings he sported tarnished with blood. That he could clean off. It wouldn't be the first time he'd cleaned another's blood from his skin, rings, or clothes. It also wasn't the first time a man lay lifeless at his feet by his own hand. The fact his brothers from the MC had their panties in a twist caused him to pause.

"Fubar, do you know who the fuck that is?" Grimm asked as he ran his large hand over his face.

The world was a swirl around Fubar as he came back to the here and now. He couldn't even tell people where he went when his mind blanked and rage took over. Features were sharpening as he tried his best to locate the trigger. What had him barreling out of the Sin City Revue the way he had? A woman, crying out for help. One of their dancers maybe? Scanning the circle of men and women that had gathered, he could see Chardonnay, one of the newer girls, with a busted lip being consoled by Bullet, one of their members.

It was obvious she had gotten knocked around by the darkening under her left eye. Was it her scream? He'd been going out for a moment of fresh air before taking a pull on a vape, a nasty habit, one that allowed him a stick to fidget with when too many thoughts were piling up in his head. Not like he could pull out one of those spinners or popping things in the bar. A vape with a little THC inside to quiet the voices appeared normal when he wasn't.

"You sure he's dead?" Fubar questioned, toeing at the man's stagnant body. He flipped his hand up and down a few times as if he were a puppeteer and could make the man dance again with the pull of a string.

"Yeah, that happens when you repeatedly slam a man's head into pavement," Preacher said, his face tightening into a pinched expression.

Flexing and extending his fingers, Fubar could feel the ache that came from fists to a face, not body slamming. Maybe his hands had gotten in the way.

"Well, who the fuck is he?" Fubar finally asked, knowing

knowledge was power, and right now he was basically a scolded puppy with Grimm holding a rolled-up newspaper set for his nose.

"Mario Mancinni, he's on the short list for the next round of made guys in the Brambilla family."

"How the fuck was I supposed to know?" he snapped like it was Grimm's fault he'd attacked a fucking member of the mob, a group they had a tenuous relationship with in Vegas to begin with. Written and unwritten rules applied, but at least with the Sin City MC, there was a good chance they were wearing a cut on their back saying *Hey, don't fuck with this guy*. Jesus, a cheap suit with good shoes wasn't a uniform claiming a set.

"Known or not," Grimm said, his face becoming firm in a way Fubar understood.

"I'm leaving, aren't I?"

"That depends." His Prez crouched by the man as others formed a wall for those rolling into the Sin City Revue for the show so they wouldn't see the man on the ground. Most in Vegas knew to look the other way when the Sinners gathered. True to form, not one head so much as glanced over to them as Grimm asked the fateful question: "You wanna live?"

* * *

"All I'm saying, Pops, is you need to consider it." Shelby Griffin did her best to not use the firm voice that had her labeled as *angry* in contrast to her male counterparts, who got the moniker *assertive and take-charge*. Three years in the corporate world had given her a look at how she didn't want business to be run.

Shelby had come back to the old neighborhood to help her grandfather. Bo Griffin was showing her the other side of business—the small, mismanaged side—and she wondered how the man had made enough to feed and clothe six children and send them all to college off of the profits from the garage he owned. He had a loyal following and probably even had a few he could show records of oil changes for since the early eighties. That aside, none of her uncles, aunts, or cousins wanted to be mechanics.

It was hard work, backbreaking most days, and the electronics in cars now, they were practically robots that moved you around. The trade he'd mastered was disappearing. Her grandfather's words, not hers because she knew mechanics would always be needed. He'd probably be disgusted by the fact when she shopped for a vehicle, it was about monthly payments and having AC and a decent Bluetooth connection. Sure, she'd bring him with when she shopped for a used vehicle, but that was years ago, before she could afford one with a warranty.

Now as she stared into the brown eyes that had faded a bit from cataracts leaving a misty aura in the iris, she couldn't force herself to strong-arm the man. While her father spoke of fearing him, Pops was the kind and gentle grandfather you wanted. Sure, his hair had turned snow white at this point, and wrinkles defined the corners of his eyes, but to her, he was the same vibrant man who'd let her air up tires at five. Calloused hands cleaned free of grease and dirt only when it was time to eat were now becoming swollen and gnarled a bit from arthritis.

"Let me see, they want to tear it down, leaving this place a car driver's nightmare."

"No, that's 980," she quipped, having always hated that strip of interstate.

"People in this neighborhood need someone they can trust to repair their car and keep them moving. Who's gonna do that if I'm gone?"

"Oh, I'm sorry, Pops, I didn't know you were immortal. Shoot, keep this place going until we're all flying spaceships and taking transporters."

"You know what I mean," he admonished. "I would feel horrible seein' my friends going to some janklegged place with corporate sales goals and fresh-pressed coveralls. Never trust a mechanic who ain't dirty at the end of the day."

"I know, Pops," she said with a sigh. "But this money they are offering—"

"All money ain't good money." His voice was becoming stern, and even with the weight of a few slow months, she could tell this wasn't the moment. "Now, if you don't mind, I need to get back in there with Marvin and Tito so we can lower this engine back in the Buick."

Shelby walked out of the office and gave Marvin a nod to step away from the register. Marvin Burk was in his midforties and had worked for her grandfather since she was a little kid. His smallish frame had added only a little pot to his belly, but he was still the same man she remembered passing her Dum-Dum suckers when she came to visit after school. Little had she considered at the time the fact Bo's Fill-Up and Fix-Up was actually her after-school daycare.

Back then her grandmother ran the register, and Shelby

would help with pushing buttons on it for those who weren't in a rush. She'd known how to turn on pumps and could be distracted for hours restocking shelves and organizing extra products in the back. It was twisted the way she could memorize barcodes and easily link them with the product. Who needed the description on the package when you knew the twelve-inch wiper blades ended in one, five, seven?

While she had loving memories of the Fill and Fix, it didn't change the fact the shop had barely broke even the last five years, and this year wasn't getting any better for them. Electric vehicles were becoming more and more popular, and those required extra certification to repair. Older cars were being tricked out and needed chop shop–type customization. Gone were the days of the minivans and sedans needing a blown gasket fixed.

At least her grandfather had allowed her to update his software a decade ago when she was in school learning about accounting. He no longer could pass a few bucks to day laborers, and every repair was now quoted, with the few mechanics he had on staff tracking their hours. All of it made her payroll run easier since her grandfather paid by the service, not by the hour.

The familiar ring of bells older than she was had her lifting her eyes enough to see a set of bikers coming into the front, where they had snacks, parts, and coffee she couldn't believe people actually drank from time to time. While the club that moved in a few decades ago none of the members had never threatened her grandparents, still she couldn't help the unease each time they came to the shop. Much like her grandfather's garage, the men of Sin City MC were a staple in the neighborhood. They had always made her feel on guard even though she'd watched many rise through the ranks over the years.

"Bo here?" a man with a squared jaw and deep tone asked.

She glanced at his cut and understood the group well enough to know Toad was a road name. Behind him, a smaller man with the presence of a giant was picking over the snack cakes. She knew him and his name of King, more importantly his rank of President.

"He's in the shop. You here to pick up a vehicle?" she asked, trying to be courteous.

"Nah, dropping off," he said, hitching his thumb over his shoulder. "My brother here blew a hose or something on the way into town. Needs his bike looked at."

"I can get Marvin," she offered, only to get a cold stare from Toad as if the idea of it was ludicrous.

"Bo's on the sign, Bo is who we deal with," Toad said as his friend set off a set of bells and so much more as he came into the building spinning his keys on his index finger.

The man didn't wear a Prospect patch, but she knew she'd never seen him before. This man was all sorts of sin wrapped up in a model-worthy body. If she worked in advertising, he would be her go-to man for any and all things she wanted to sell to women. His eyes were an icy blue, lips full, and skin a tawny suntan gold. Did his ass have a soundtrack playing as he walked in all slow-motion like a movie dream? She swore she heard the song "Freak Me" playing as he strode in and cut his eyes at her with a smirk that nearly took out her knees.

Stop it, Shelby, your ass knows better, she scolded herself internally. At least she thought it was internally, until Toad's brow furrowed and a low chuckle let her know she'd at least mouthed the words if not said them out loud.

"Jesus, Fubar, you could make a nun change religions."

Fubar caught his keys in his hand from the quick spin, then looked dumbfounded at Toad. "What'd I do?" he questioned, completely oblivious to Shelby's statement.

"Nothin'. So Bo?" Toad prodded.

"Right, I'll get him." Shelby opened the door to the shop as a mixture of whirring noises and the stagnant smell of oil and grease rushed her, setting her to rights for half a second as she moved around Marvin, who was doing checks on a newer-model Ford with the computer.

The pully system her grandfather was overseeing with one of the younger mechanics, Tito, was lowering in a V-8 engine block in the third bay of the garage. She knew to stay back as he guided in the heavy chunk of steel so he could begin ratcheting it in place.

"Pops," she called once he'd started the process. "There's a biker out here who insists—"

"You don't want to do that," the key-twirling Adonis said as he moved around her, his hand gently touching her shoulder to make room, but all it did was set off a blaze of heat through her shirt. A light smell of teak and leather made her head swim a bit as she did her best to brace herself.

What was wrong with her? He was a good-looking man. She'd seen attractive men before. Sure, most were on the other side of a screen, but damn, she was fangirling over a damn biker. She was closer to thirty than twenty and needed to act like a damn grown-up.

"What don't I want to do?" Pops replied. "Because I know a

man who ain't my employee isn't back in an area where I have liability."

"My bad," the man said as she recalled Toad calling him Fubar. "Just wondering how long this car was sitting up waiting on an engine."

"A week, why?" Pops stood back and began scanning the interior of the open hood.

"You need a cat."

"Boy, do you like talking in riddles?"

Shelby's gaze shifted between the two men as Fubar motioned to Tito to winch up the engine again. The mechanic waited for the nod from Pops before making the chains lift the block.

"If I may," Fubar said, waiting for approval before reaching down on the side where her grandfather was standing. She shifted, trying to see what his hands were doing, but the dangling engine was in her way.

A minute later he lifted out a cottony leaf-and-stick nest and set it outside the door. She leapt as a mouse took off first back into the garage, only to turn around when Fubar stomped his booted foot a few times, sending the rodent back across the road and into a grass patch.

"How the heck did I miss that?" Pops said, scratching the side of his head.

His cataracts were getting worse, but Tito didn't even wear glasses. He should have caught that. Glancing over her shoulder, she wondered how Fubar could have seen it through the glass window behind the register. Three open bays and he figured out there was a nest in a car.

"I was lucky he stole some white fluff, or I would have

missed it too," Fubar said. "Bright white was a harsh contrast. You must be Bo."

"Yeah, you the one who wants to talk to me?"

"Yes, sir. I don't have my tools here, so I need someone to fix a few hoses that had more damage than I thought before I left Vegas."

"Vegas, that's a decent ride," Pops said. "You visiting from the mother chapter?"

"Something like that," Fubar said as he gave a quick glance to Shelby before the two walked out to the parking lot. It took everything in her to not follow.

Jesus, the man had her practically mewing. She hoped Pops would get him fixed up and on his way quick, because she wasn't sure she could control herself around him, and refused to be accountable for her actions. Thankfully the man was singularly focused on his bike.

"You need to borrow my Carmex?" Marvin held out the white glass container with the yellow lid.

"Why?" she questioned, coming out of her lust-filled gaze.

"You keep biting your lip like it's chapped."

Shelby cut her eyes at him. "You need to mind your business."

"I thought you gave up bad boys when that DB you dated in high school got a two hundred on his SATs."

"That's not why I broke up with him," she lied. "That would have been shallow."

Shallow was the fact she was dating him because he had an eight-pack in high school, and she tried to delude herself into believing deep down he was intelligent. Brains were her turn-on for long-term guys. A minimum of a six-pack, killer smile, and swagger were for her one-and-dones, the ones she could look back on fondly because she knew the backbreaking orgasms were the one thing men like him excelled in. Sadly, spelling his name correctly on a standard test seemed to be a struggle.

"Young lady, I've known you from the time your hormones spiked," he said. "Watched your mama, daddy, and grandparents make the sign of the cross more times than I can count."

"Guess we know why I never went after you," she countered even though the man was practically a young uncle to her.

"Whatever, youngblood. I know you, Shelby, and that man has you biting your bottom lip."

"I am not," she said, turning on her heel and heading back to the front, where King was waiting at the counter with three Swiss Rolls. "Got a sweet tooth today?"

"What can I say," he said, pulling out a few bills and passing them to her. "Gotta keep my energy up. We tend to have long nights when friends come to town."

This time Shelby recognized the bite to her lower lip and forced herself to release. Everything, including the man's name, said he was a mistake. A fuckup beyond all recognition. He was a walking red flag, and she knew better. If only her brains would talk to other parts of her body.

When Fubar strode back in with her grandfather, he was wearing mirrored aviators, and she caught sight of herself. Had she completely forgotten she was wearing one of the shop's starched button-down shirts with an embroidered name tag like all the men wore? The short-sleeve navy blue top was all about imagination since it didn't show a single curve she might possess. Her hair was styled into a no-nonsense bitch bun, her normally curly dark locks smoothed back to the point you would assume they didn't have so much as a body wave let alone the practical ringlets she had. Damn, she should go take up Marvin's offer of Carmex. At least she'd have something on her face.

"Dang, I missed that crack starting," Fubar said as they approached the counter.

"The one on the side of your head?" Toad joked and set a bag of chips and an energy drink on the counter, reminding Shelby she was there to check out customers.

"Good thing you came in when you did," Pops said. "Good thing I can get the parts by this afternoon."

"Bad thing?" King questioned as he opened one of the packages and took out a roll.

"Bad thing is, I probably couldn't start working on it until the end of next week," Pops said. "I know y'all want me to do the work and not one of my men, but I've got vehicles ahead of you, and this one is making me take days off to go to the doctor."

"I'm nothing if not an inconvenience." Shelby passed Toad his change as Fubar leaned an arm on the counter and began playing with the battery-operated fans. They were a mix of superheroes and mythical creatures like mermaids and unicorns.

"How long does it take to go to the doctor?" King asked.

"A few days when you put it off for forty years," she countered, not about to be questioned when it came to her grandfather's health. "And I swear to God, if you try the whole sob story about a lost little boy needing his vroom-vroom machine being more important, you will not like the end result."

"Am I the little boy?" Fubar questioned, finally breaking the trance he had from the spinning foam fan blades. "I'm not in too much of a hurry. But I could fix it since you're getting the parts, if you didn't mind. I'll do it in the driveway so I'm not in your liability space."

"I don't know." Pops rubbed the side of his face the way he did when he was getting worried.

"How is it any different than me going to a parts store?" Fubar asked. "If you hadn't made these guys codependent on you because you do good work, they would actually have the tools I need to fix it myself."

"California has regulations, Nevada doesn't, son."

"Then you can inspect it before I take your beautiful granddaughter for a ride to make sure it's running right."

Shelby shifted, about to protest because how the hell had she been pulled into this negotiation, when Toad held up his hand. "Don't even try, Shelby. Many tried, and all have failed."

"Fine, I'll pay you to have me fix it," Fubar said, sweetening the deal. "I normally do my own maintenance."

"And you missed that crack," Pops asserted.

"That crack can't be more than a few hundred miles old." Fubar then turned his icy blue stare to Shelby, sending electricity across her skin to the point she feared electrocution. "What do you think, darlin'? You think I can make my bike safe enough for a ride?"

"I filled out my organ donor card, doesn't mean I want to become one this week, thank you." The protest was more for Toad's assumption she lacked the ability to say no to Fubar. As if she were one of the Angels down at the Sinners' clubhouse down to fuck with little more than a glance from a man in a cut.

"Me too, we could save twenty-six lives, or just our own," he said as his hand reached across the counter and gently lifted hers. The back of her fingers grazed his lips, and thank God her other hand was flat on the counter to keep her from completely collapsing. "I'm Daniel, by the way."

"Thought your name was Fubar." The words came out harsh because she had to force them over a hard lump making her throat scratchy.

"That's only for people who've known me for more than twenty-four hours. Don't worry, darlin'. I'm pretty sure you'll kick my shiftless ass to the curb before then."

"It's Shelby," she said if for no other reason than she couldn't help the panty-wetting way the man let *darlin'* roll over his tongue. She was sure she wasn't the first and wouldn't be the last woman he used the affectionate nickname on, but deep down she wanted to be special to him. "And you've already lost thirty minutes on that clock, Daniel."

two

"DAMN, man, you pulled out the government name on the woman," Xavier "Toad" Carmichael said as they walked backed to their bikes. Fubar realized he'd have to go butts to nuts or walk the two blocks back to the clubhouse as Shelby took down the VIN number for his vehicle for the parts order.

"I'm more impressed with the fact Bo didn't knock the back of his head with the a tire iron," King said as he straddled his bike. "That's what I would have done."

"We talked engines," Fubar said, then glanced back at the woman with a starched cotton shirt tucked in at the waist making her dangerous curves more pronounced. All he could do was wonder if the headlights were as decorative as the chassis. "It's bonding."

"Bonding is one thing. Being allowed to speak to Shelby Griffin beyond a transaction is another." Toad started up his bike, then gave Fubar a snarl as if to say, *You ain't riding bitch to me.* "I'll see you back at the clubhouse."

"Try to not fuck up until you're back on Sinners ground," King said, and Fubar gave him a nod.

It wasn't as if he meant to fuck things up. If his parents had actually agreed with the doctors when he was younger and put him on meds, there was at least a 20 percent chance he might have learned the coping skills to redirect his wandering mind. Instead his mind was focusing, along with another part of him, toward Shelby.

"What's the damage going to be?" Fubar asked as she stood with a tablet, tapping through screens with one of those white plastic pencils that worked on touch screens.

"How hot was it in Vegas when you left?" She squatted down to get the serial number for the engine case. Her dark mahogany skin shimmered a bit in the sunlight with her dark hair smoothed up and restrained.

"See, the thing about Vegas is the heat is a dry heat," he joked, and she turned slightly as a curl escaped her bun and landed on the side of her face. He instantly followed the swirl of hair with his eyes, finding himself feeling as if he were sliding down and coming to rest at her lips.

When she tucked the loose strand behind her ear, he was shook and needed to remember the task at hand—giving money, cash of course, because swiping a card was the quickest way to be found after a phone's SIM card.

"It's impressive," Shelby said as she stood.

"You got X-ray vision there, darlin'?" he questioned, and her lips became a firm line.

"The crack on the engine case. How fast were you hauling out of Vegas to overheat it this bad?"

"Not fast enough, I should have met you before that chip grew on your shoulder," he said. "Who hurt you?"

"No one. And trust me, Fubar"—she said his name by drawing it out and anchoring it to anger—"you may have charmed my pops, but he's got bad eyes and a penchant to trust."

"And you?"

"Twenty-twenty." She tapped her temple with the stylus.

"You know twenty-ten is actually perfect vision," he countered, the way he tended to blurt facts to correct a person who didn't need correcting. He found most were offended by his so-called back talk. In Vegas, the Sinners seemed to pause now when people stated facts, as if waiting for him to, at the minimum, amend the comment.

"Are you an ophthalmologist as well as a shade tree mechanic?"

"I pay attention to things, the little ones most overlook," he said, stepping closer to her as he did his best to read the vibe she was giving him. For most women it was *Fuck me, daddy*, and it made it easier on him since he'd always had a problem with social cues. "I don't always understand or lock them in, in the moment, like the fact your name is on your shirt, so you probably think I'm either illiterate or ignorant. That's fine, most do, but I'm not."

There was a slight furrow in her brow, and while he knew how to charm women, he didn't want to entrance her with a smile and few genuinely spoken words. That was what the women he slept with didn't understand. When he spoke, there wasn't malice. He enjoyed a beautiful female until his anxiety set in as things progressed. He could play the role of neurotypical for long enough to get past his satisfaction and even hers. The calming wash of chemicals poured over his brain, of endorphins, oxytocin, and testosterone, setting him to rights. Then there was the after, the thinking, the processing, the comedown, as it were, and he feared the same rejection of his quirks and fell into a role.

"Okay, well, Pops said if you're using his tools and space, it will require a deposit," she said. "Something about the name on your chest has him a little skeptical."

"Understood."

"Great, so the part is going to be a grand for a new one, plus the hoses and the deposit." Worrying her lower lip, she tapped a few times on her tablet. "I'll round it up. Twenty-five hundred will hold it all for you. I'm assuming it will be on a card?"

"No, I have cash," he said, then glanced around the neighborhood and headed into the shop's convenience store area before removing the wad tucked into his inner pocket.

He may be dumb, but he wasn't stupid. The Sinners had a reputation. People tended to notice newbies, and even if he'd partied a time or two over the years in Oakland, he was fresh meat. It might be worth it to someone to try. Lord knows he'd been the moron who'd done that in the past. Acting without thinking, he could trademark that shit.

Fubar counted out the hundreds and passed her the stack, and she quickly crouched behind the counter, causing him to lean over. She was putting the cash in a timed safe with a drop feature. The view of her heart-shaped ass caused him to lose sight of what she was doing with the cash. It wasn't hard. Her hips tapered out in a way that, from the aerial view he had, it would have been impossible to not make out the divot between her ass cheeks.

"Anything else we can help you with?" Bo said as he cleared his throat, making Shelby glance up and spy him practically planking on the counter.

"No, sir," he said, righting himself.

"Then be on your way. You can come back tomorrow and start working on your bike."

"Marvin will have the place open at eight," Shelby said.

"And you?" Fubar asked.

"Will be with me all day," Bo said as the congenial guy he'd been talking to shifted into the protective grandfather mode.

Or maybe he'd misread how the old man had been with him when they were inspecting the bike. Were Toad and King right, that he'd crossed a line with his comments to Shelby? Taking all the facts into account, he gave the Griffins a quick nod and headed back to the clubhouse. It wasn't so much he hadn't been taught about social graces over the years. He'd had it beaten into him, literally, but bruises heal, and memories fade. Sure, he could remember the Pythagorean theorem and all of the noble gases. But he could never master the "I before E" rule because of conflicting realities. There was *science*, *seize*, *weird*, and *feisty*, to name a few, and if he didn't get distracted quick, he'd go through the whole dictionary in an attempt to prove why living in society shouldn't have rules.

People should straight up tell each other how they feel without drawing it out and playing games. He wanted to fix his bike. He also wanted to give Shelby a ride. One was acceptable to say out loud, while the other was taboo. It was too bold to be up-front and simply say, *I like you, let's fuck*. At the same time, women would whine because they wanted to know his intentions, what he wanted, and say he's closed off.

Again his father's fists were to blame. Better to be considered a fool than open his mouth and get the shit knocked out of him for daring to speak the truth.

"Fubar," Jean-Mathieu "Frenchie" Lévesque called, making him take in a few of the buildings of the industrial area before turning around. "Man, they should have called you Dazed and Confused."

"It wouldn't fit on the patch," Fubar replied automatically before recognizing the joke. He walked toward the clubhouse dragging a key he wore around his neck back and forth. The sensation and sound of the stainless steel balls of the chain gave him a landing point. "Waldo was floated around because I never knew where I was."

"I'm sure." With a hard slap to his back, Frenchie and he walked into the bar section.

The mix of pounding bass from the loud music grounded Fubar enough that he wasn't overwhelmed by all the people. Angels, the club girls, were using their charms to find the bed they'd be lying in that night. Similar to the dancers at the Revue in Vegas. He liked the fact they were up-front in what they wanted, usually a hard drink followed by a harder fuck. Most figured Fubar was too dense to think beyond that moment and left him alone after they got theirs. In many ways that was the perfect relationship for him.

He wasn't Ice with an Ol' Lady and kids, with more on the way. Fubar had grown up in what the world considered the nuclear family based on the post-bomb-being dropped society. Mom and Dad in the home with a sister and brother, all willing to disown and ignore his existence because he had been an issue. Tough love was the name of his father's game, and no one was to step out of line. Those who did got the back of his hand until they were old enough to handle his fist.

"Hey Fubar," one of the Angels said as she brought him a beer. Clad in leather tied tight to push up her breasts, she twisted her finger on the end of her long ponytail.

"A little early, don't you think?" he said, though most of the men were already drinking.

"I got it," Frenchie said. "The choirboy here has to keep his wits about him."

"Oh, was he a bad boy?" the woman purred, and she reached for the key he was dragging on the chain, only to have him catch her wrist with his other hand.

"No." The order was quick, firm, and would become a grapevine rumor among the Angels.

Frenchie cut his eyes at him with a warning glare. They knew of Fubar, but didn't know him. Few did, but his reputation was known among all chapters. When wronged, the hair trigger in him snapped, and few could stop him. Why should they be able to? He couldn't.

* * *

"Pops, I better not find you in the kitchen," Shelby called as she used the key to unlock his front door. "Your surgery is in three hours."

"I know, I know," he grumbled as hanger from lack of a good breakfast reared its ugly head.

The home brought back so many memories from growing

up, probably because little had changed in the place since the eighties. While twenty years ago her grandparents had all the boys of the family come over and update the siding from white to a pale yellow, little else was different. Wood paneling still covered the walls, now cluttered with pictures fading a bit behind the dust-covered glass. The linoleum needed to be replaced in the kitchen because it was peeling a bit, but that was for another time according to her grandfather. Maybe when his vision wasn't so cloudy, he'd see the need.

Giving a smile to her grandmother's picture, prominently placed on the side table next to the recliner that gave the one from *Frasier* a run for its money, she stripped off the current blanket covering it and swapped it out with another before heading to the laundry room to add the old one to the pile.

"No one said to do that, girl," Pops scolded.

"It'll give me something to do when I'm here this week."

"This week, you know this is too much of a burden to be putting on you."

"Oh, yeah, it's cutting into my social season something fierce." Her lips pursed as she tried her best to not laugh. "I'll have to wait until I get home to watch my shows because you don't have a smart TV."

"Does it turn on and make noise while showing people moving around?" he queried. "Sounds smart enough for me. Last thing I need is some newfangled TV with government probes peering into my house."

"Want your phone?" Shelby passed him the standard person-tracking device most used and tried to not be a snot about the irony.

"It's not right for a girl your age to still be single." He snatched the phone from her.

"Didn't you marry Nana at twenty-eight?"

"I was twenty-eight. She was twenty-five."

"And?"

"And I'm telling you she wasn't right in the head." He chuckled a bit, causing Shelby to shake her head at his foolishness.

"I won't be the only one here all weekend. Connie, Terrence, and my folks will be coming through too." At least her siblings were close enough to come down and give her a reprieve from sitting around at the house.

"Why won't you be here?" he questioned, narrowing his eyes at her. "You're not thinking of going out with that biker, are you? I saw the way he was looking at you."

"That you saw?" she snickered. "Might need to get your hearing tested. You didn't even raise an eyebrow at what he said to me."

"What did he say?"

She hustled on the light jacket her grandfather insisted on wearing as she walked him to her car, making sure to lock the door behind them. He hated when she doted on him like an invalid, so she didn't guide him into the seat or buckle him in like she would have to after the surgery.

"What did he say that was so bad? I'll call Marvin right now and tell him to not let the kid touch my tools," Pops grumbled as she got on the interstate to get over to the hospital.

"You didn't take your blood thinners today, did you?" she asked, going through the checklist given to her by the doctor. Her avoidance technique wasn't working. Sure, he was blind, but her grandfather could see things most couldn't, and he knew his grandchildren well enough to smell her deception.

While Fubar's attentions were nice, she liked the idea of being protected by someone. Even if it was her grandfather. Maybe she spent too much time watching movies and TV growing up and believed the men in her life were supposed to bully anyone who approached her to see if they were worthy of her.

"Shelby Anne," he warned.

"You didn't hear it, so it didn't happen. I'm just a little bit crazy, it seems. I probably misunderstood."

"What did you misunderstand?"

"Him asking me to help him test out his bike after it's fixed," she said.

"That boy is simple," her grandfather replied. "He may run with those men, but after talking to him, I honestly think he only wanted to test his motorcycle."

"What do you mean, simple?" she questioned, now replaying their whole interaction the day before, thinking she'd missed something vital in the conversation. He had been flirting with her, hadn't he?

"I don't know. That's what we called it when I was young." Pops shifted nervously in his seat. "Look, there are some men that know their right from their left and can strip an engine down to the plugs without even thinking about it. That's the Fubar character. Doesn't mean they know when to stop. Like that guy in the Steinbeck book, what's-his-name." With a few snaps of his fingers, he pulled the memory from somewhere deep in the recesses of his mind. *"Of Mice and Men."*

"You think Fubar is like Lennie? A sweet guy, but doesn't know when to stop petting the bunnies?"

"Not that bad, but Shelby, be careful."

"Pops, I'd never date a biker."

"Oh Lord, she said never. We all know what that means."

"What does it mean?" she questioned, pulling into the parking ramp and tossing her car into park.

"It means you're going to," he grumbled. "I've raised six children, four of which were girls, and I know good, darn well that when they say never, they are fighting with themselves to not do it. But they will."

"Only the girls do that?"

"Oh, them boys too, like your daddy saying he was never going to talk to your mother."

"So when you say you'll never sell the shop," she said, flipping the question back to what really needed to be addressed and not just because he'd been putting off this surgery for nearly three years already. The man was closer to eighty than seventy. He should be at the shop talking crap to the mechanics and driving the new owner crazy with his stories. Not trying to drop a new engine in a damn Buick. "That means you're ready to."

"I knew your parents made a mistake when they let you learn how to read," he mumbled and fought with the seat belt to get out. "Teaching a girl to read means they're gonna have thoughts, and then look what happens."

Stilling his hands with her own, she unbuckled the seat belt, giving him a knowing look.

"Don't you give me your Anne eyes," he warned, narrowing his lids to her.

MICHEL PRINCE

"Nana gave them to my daddy, and he gave them to me," she said. "That's the way it works sometimes."

"Shelby, I appreciate your concern, but once I get these floaters gone, I won't miss nests, and I won't have to feel to get the right size. I'll simply pull out the socket wrench."

"It's more than your eyes, Pops. I can see how stiff you are at the end of the day, and I can only imagine how hard it is in the morning to get out of bed. You've earned a rest."

"Those companies offering money want my land, not my shop." Tears were filling his eyes, and she knew she shouldn't have started right before surgery. After stepping out of the car, she rushed around to help him and make sure he saw the curbs. "I built that place. There are more than memories there. A community depends on me."

"Don't go getting upset," she said, pulling a tissue from her purse and dabbing at the corners of his eyes. "I'll stop pushing. I will."

"Today maybe, but what about tomorrow?"

"Tomorrow too, I'll give you until next week before I circle back."

"Shoot, and you're gonna have me all drugged up for half of it. That's not fair," he said. "Let's push the surgery back another week."

"No." The firmness was enough for his shoulders to slump a bit, as if she were his parent and not his grandchild giving a command, as she approached the receptionist. "Hello, I'm checking Beauregard Griffin in for surgery."

Four hours later the nurse was wheeling her grandfather out to Shelby's car, and the two of them wrangled him into the front seat. He wore dark shades, the kind not letting a sliver of daylight in, and groggily mumbled a protest about something or another.

"They blinded me," he cried out, and she placed a hand on his.

"No, Pops, you're wearing dark glasses, and we need to keep your eyes covered until I can get you to bed."

"My chair, I'll sleep in my chair."

"Is it a recliner?" the nurse asked, and Shelby nodded. "Then it's fine. Alright, Mr. Griffin, I'm going to need you to rest, and we'll see you back in a week for a checkup."

"Like hell you will."

"Pops," Shelby scolded.

"It's okay," the nurse said, closing the door to the car. Her lanyard covered in pins about positivity and team spirit were just for show at this point, Shelby figured. "I'm used to it, been escorting out old men for over a decade. Follow the instructions for aftercare, and call us if there are any issues."

"Thank you."

Pops fell asleep a block from the hospital, and Shelby wasn't sure if she should get him home or drive around like a parent with a colicky baby. When she passed by the Fill and Fix, she saw Fubar wearing a white wifebeater tank, worn-in jeans, and ass-kicking boots. He must have been there for a while if the suntanned skin glistening with sweat was any indication. While most of the Sinners she saw were covered in tats, what she could see of his skin was clear, each muscle on his arm outlined as he stood to take a break. Setting the mechanical socket wrench down, he guzzled from a bottle of water before turning slightly to capture her with his eyes. He twisted the top, then pointed to something in front of her.

The hard slam of her brakes as she stopped just slightly into the lane for cross traffic woke Pops with a jolt. He grabbed her arm that she'd slammed onto his chest as if that would have saved him flying through the window. Her heart thundered in her chest, and heat burned through her body, and while she wanted to thank Fubar for knocking her right, she didn't need the temptation of looking at him.

"Good God, what was that," Pops said, patting around blindly.

"A dog," she lied, not wanting to admit she was practically panting over Fubar and nearly ran a stop sign. Good thing no one was parked near the end of the block. She had drifted as if she were going to turn. "We're almost home."

"Was it the Cruzes down the street's dog? That poor mangy mutt gets out all the time."

"No, I don't think so. It ran off." Keeping with the lie was the only way to get out of the absurdity of the situation as she tried to remember what kind of dog the Cruzes had. "It was a shaggy gray dog."

"You should go look for it after you drop me off. It's probably been lost for a while."

"You want me to leave you at home and go chasing after a stray dog?" she questioned finally pulling up in front of his house.

"What else are you going to do? Putter around chasing after me in case I lift the remote that's too heavy for me now?"

"Ten pounds, Pop, that's it. Please stop making this a big deal."

"I ain't taken more than two days away from the shop, and you want me to stay here a week listening to TV."

"Rest a few days," she said guiding him into his old recliner and turning on the TV. "Then I'll take you to the shop so you can yell at the mechanics, but only if you promise to behave."

"Treating me like a seven-year-old. I'm a grown man."

"Who should know better," she bit back. "Now, you hungry?"

"Yes, I'm hungry. I'm near starvation at this point."

"Then listen to your scores, and I'll make you a sandwich."

Shelby shook her head as she moved around the kitchen where she'd learned to cook. Her nana would be livid if she saw how out of sorts it was. Clean, sure, but Pops didn't have the same need to have the staples around as her nana did. Run out of mustard, there was at least one if not two bottles in the pantry. Fruit was always available on the table and never rotted. Lord knows how long those bananas had been sitting on the counter, but they were past the time even she would have made bread from them.

At least the lunch meat and cheese seemed fresh as she made him up a sandwich, poured some chips on the plate, and used a fork to get two pickle spears out of the jar. With a tall glass of cooled water, she added a little sugar-free pink lemonade powder to flavor it and brought the lunch to him.

"You still awake?" she asked softly, hoping the man had drifted back to sleep.

"My stomach won't shut up, so yeah, I'm up," he grumbled, and she helped him feel the plate.

Once he was eating, she went back into the kitchen and took stock. Shelby could hear her grandmother speaking to her while she used her phone to order everything she needed from the grocery store to stock the house right.

• • •

"Tell me how many cans of navy beans we have left?" Nana called as Shelby balanced on the step stool in the pantry and counted the cans.

"Two."

"Stewed tomatoes?"

"Four."

"Okay, do we have any bags of flour?"

"No, Nana," Shelby said. "Nana, why do you always have more than you need?"

"Because, sweet Shelby, we're the home where people come for shelter, and I never want to make people feel as if they are a burden because I have to run to the store." Her nana cradled her face with her soft hands. "When people come hat in hand, I don't want them to think they are putting us out. If I have the basics, I can always whip something up."

"But why do they come to you?" she asked.

"Why shouldn't they, baby?" Nana offered a sweet smile. "God blessed me with the ability to help others. It would be wrong for me to be selfish."

"So Daddy should be giving money to the guys on the off-ramps?"

"I think he gives of himself when he can."

There was no flour in the pantry. The bit of sugar was so old it was clumping. She'd been with her pops at the shop, but only came by sparingly to the house. It had been years since she'd grabbed anything from the pantry, and when she moved a storage container, she found the spot where her nana had kept the full-size candy bars. Anytime the grocery store had a "buy three or five" for a discount, she would triple down. Lifting one of the Snickers, she flipped it over and saw the expiration date was nearly five years past.

Shelby dumped the rest of the bars in the trash and sent a group text to her cousins. She couldn't call out her aunts and uncles, but cousins were on her level, and they all needed to step up. No wonder Pops didn't want to sell the shop. It was the only time he got to be around people, because once Nana died, the family had slowly drifted away.

three

"YOU ALMOST DONE FOR THE DAY?" Tito asked as Fubar began putting the tools away.

He'd memorized where each one had been before utilizing them, but it appeared that, over the day, other pieces were not put back in place. Having only focused on the tools he used, it was hard for him to move the others without verifying where they should be. A trickle of sweat stung his left eye, and he quickly wiped it away. This wasn't the time for a meltdown, and he knew how that tended to sneak up on him.

"Everything has a place."

Everything but a child who doesn't put his socks in the same drawer as his underwear. Dear Lord, the child is an anomaly. Does he not know the inner workings of societal norms? What will others think?

Dragging his key along the chain around his neck, he stood frozen, unable to make the decision for fear of rejection. As if putting a screwdriver in the wrong place would be an issue.

One would think after years of being a Sinner, he'd be able to see the way he was raised wasn't how most of society behaved.

"*Quit focusing on the problems you can't solve,*" the high school librarian Ms. Blomquist said as he sat in study hall unable to move past question number two. "*Daniel, move past it, and try to answer all of the ones you can, then circle back. Nothing in the rules states you have to respond to question two before question twenty-one.*"

The overwhelming sense of relief he'd had in that moment was such that he broke through one of the hardest walls trapping him into a small area. Special Ed students, ones with dyslexia, reading comprehension problems, and the like, were supposed to be given extra time. His father refused to allow him to even be tested. Instead he was the problem child at school, the one written off by most, if not all, of the teachers after a two-minute discussion around the watercooler in the break room.

"You good, man?" Tito asked, and Fubar let out a slight sigh.

"This the way Bo likes his tools?"

"No," Marvin scolded a bit. "But I gave up fixing them. Between Tito here and Bo losing his vision, it's a struggle every night."

"Losing his vision?"

"Yeah, that's where Shelby's at today," Marvin explained. "She had to take Bo to the eye doc for surgery."

"If he's having problems seeing, then we should be making sure to put things in place," Fubar reasoned. "Anything to lighten his load."

"You want to try, go for it. If you clean out the drawers,

you'll see the white outlines for the tools," Tito explained. "It's a time thing for me."

"The seconds you save tossing it randomly in a drawer are eaten up by having to dig for twenty minutes to find what you need."

Marvin tossed Fubar a bottle of 409 and a rag. "If that's what floats your boat, it makes mine sail, man. Have at it. Ain't no one gonna complain if this place was put back in order."

"Aren't you closing up soon?" he questioned.

"Yeah, you can do it in the morning if you want."

Fubar weighed the pros and cons of that offer. It was irritating him that the garage wasn't in order, but would it drive him crazy enough he wouldn't be able to sleep until it was fixed? There was a high probability of that, because he was flicking his thumb over the side of his middle finger. Twitches, they got worse when he had personal responsibility for the problem.

"Shelby would kick your ass if you left him here with the keys," Tito said.

"Who said I'd leave him?" Marvin countered. "Then again, who said you'd leave him?"

"Huh? I know Shelby wouldn't approve overtime."

"It's not overtime, and there wouldn't be need for it if you'd been doing your job right the first time," Fubar said, wishing his father's voice hadn't been part of the comment.

"Oh, is that so? Now you're the boss man here?" Tito argued. "I know people too. You're not the only tough guy in a leather coat. This is Oakland."

"See, I wasn't going to force a situation. Then you had to run your mouth, and I don't do good with people running their mouths and thinking they are superior," Marvin warned. "Now I'm wondering exactly how much Bo needs a man like you working for him."

"Oh, so I'm fired now? Bullshit. I'm done for the day, and I will be back tomorrow."

"See, that just makes me want to be an asshole," Fubar said as Tito stormed away. "On that note…"

With a quick call made on the flip phone he had to use, Fubar called up the Prospects of the Oakland Chapter and within minutes the rumble of bikes echoed through the garage.

"What's up, Fubar?" Rubble asked as he took stock of the place.

"Cleanup duty." Fubar pointed to rolls of paper towels, a few brooms, and the piles of tools he and Marvin had removed from the red-and-silver metal chests while they were waiting. "Bo takes care of all of you. We're going to pay back the favor. I need the toolboxes cleaned out and sparkling, floors swept, garbage out. Marvin here will make sure any liquids that need to be recycled are in the proper bins."

"You want us to wear French maid outfits while we dust too?" Frankenstein asked. The big motherfucker had a face only a mother could love. Scarred as if he'd gone face-first through a plate glass window at least once, if not twice, in his lifetime.

"Don't tempt me," Fubar replied.

"You're just visiting, right?" Birdy, a newer Prospect, asked. The kid had to have gotten his nickname from the pointed nose and thin frame. Then again, he could be a little "cuckoo for Cocoa Puffs" crazy. One never knew for sure.

"Oh shit," Rubble said as if he could see the rage manifesting in Fubar from the implied "it wasn't his job" look on the kid's face. "He's new, boss."

"New, I was new once," Fubar said, unaware of the fist tightening around a wrench he was sporting. "Never back talked a patch higher than mine. Spoke over, pointed out shit, but never once questioned an order, and believe you me, I probably should have. In other words, get that cut below your nose fixed, or I'll give the surgeons a reason to keep it wired shut for a month."

"He's a fucking Enforcer," Rubble warned under his breath.

"Yes, sir, what do you need me to do?" Birdy asked, getting the hint as Fubar steadied himself.

Within twenty minutes, all seven of the Prospects had been assigned a task and were scrubbing away. Marvin and Fubar were grouping the tools and making sure they were in perfect running order. It was wrong the rush Fubar felt when OCD met a project. If nothing else, it was blocking out the fear of what was going on. Years ago he read a book where it said vampires could be distracted by tossing a bunch of anything on the floor: pins, grains of sugar, paper clips, a stack of paper. They physically couldn't move on until they had counted all of the pieces and knew the number. He'd never found a kinship with a creature more in his life. Now he wondered why this weakness wasn't used in more monster movies. Probably would end the scare factor for the viewer if they just had to keep Equal packets in their pocket and they were able to walk, not run, away from the nocturnal hunter.

Music blared from an old-school boom box playing the local retro station. The sun was setting on the day, and Marvin turned on the shop lights, making the Fill-Up glow in the darkness of the other industrial buildings. A neighborhood surrounded the area, and people were stopping their evening walks to take in the unusual behavior. When a black-and-white pulled in and flashed its blue-and-red lights, everyone came to a stop.

Ice trickled down Fubar's back as he put on the only uniform he ever wore, his leather cut, having taken it off because of the heat of the day. Flipping off the music brought the attention of the last of the men, who all stood taller, trying to act as if they weren't shitting their pants. Fucking Prospects, he'd wanted slave labor, and that's why he didn't even clue the officers in to his plans. Mostly because Toad and King had been fucking with him about Shelby the whole night before.

"Bo around?" a middle-aged male cop asked as he did a little head count of the group, his hands resting on his duty belt.

Fubar went all Terminator on his ass, doing an assessment of danger and catching the fact a snap on either side of his duty belt was undone. Taser and gun no longer had a restriction on them.

"He had surgery today," Marvin said. "The guys from the neighborhood were doing a little community service."

"Community service, huh?" The cop surveyed the garage, and Fubar saw a glow on his partner's face in the vehicle. Probably running plates on all the bikes in the lot. More than likely his Nevada ones were first on the list.

"Bo did me a solid," Fubar said. "I called in the guys to help me do a deep clean so when he came back, it was nice."

"Looks more like you're taking Bo's inventory?" The

narrowing of the cop's eyes had Fubar stepping forward to square up with him. "Enforcer, huh?"

"Yeah, we're practically twins." Fubar's head tilted to the side. "My dad's in your gang. Think of us as cousins, and give your family the benefit of the doubt."

"You're a Sinner, last thing I see is family."

"Too bad."

The air cooled around Fubar, and he could see the world starting to fade away. Why was it when he tried to do the right thing, people assumed the worst? Sure, most times they were right, but damn, give the man a chance to fuck up before saying he did. The numbness in his fingers matched the light-headed feeling, and he wondered if he was going to be able to stop himself before he pulled a him and fucked up his life beyond repair. Grimm had been willing to send him to Oakland for shelter. King didn't want his bullshit to bring attention to the local chapter, and Lord knows police were the biggest gang in the country.

"Fubar?" Shelby's voice bit through the fog, and he extended his flexed fingers. She was in more comfortable clothing, leggings and a longer tank top stretching near the top even with the sports bra trying to crush her breasts. Her hair was pulled up, but unlike the "don't fuck with me" bun, a bundle of curls were resting on the crown of her head. "Marvin? What is going on here?"

"That's what we were determining, ma'am," the officer said. "You're Bo's granddaughter, right?"

"Yes, Shelby Griffin." She stepped into the shop area and took stock of the current mess that had to happen right before everything was put back in place. "My grandfather is resting. I took the call from your dispatcher about a break-in at the shop. A really bad one by the looks of it."

"It got a little out of hand," Marvin admitted as he stood by the worktable where he was matching up charging stations with power tools.

"I see that," she said. "Marvin's our employee. I'm assuming nothing is missing?"

"Shoot, we found a half dozen things Bo had been looking for," he admitted.

"I think everything is fine. I'll have a discussion with the ringleader. Fubar, office," Shelby ordered, and Birdy oohed until Fubar picked up a wrench and tossed it at his head.

Fubar straightened up a bit, for the first time not worried about the scolding he was about to receive. In fact, he was looking forward to it.

The convenience part of the business had been locked up, so Shelby used her keys to open it up and then the office in the back. Fubar followed like a good little puppy and did his best not to be mesmerized by the curve of her ass. It was hard. Even in tennis shoes she couldn't help swishing her hips in a way that had him imagining her rocking in his arms as they danced, swinging from side to side in perfect rhythm to the song as he held her.

* * *

"You've been here one day and aren't on the payroll. What is going on?" Shelby questioned as she sat behind the desk and began opening the mail that Marvin must have tossed on there. "Is your bike fixed?"

"About that," he interjected, and she paused what she was doing waiting for the bullshit to spew from the man's mouth. "I might need a day or two. Guess the stereotyping about mechanics making up shit that's wrong with your vehicle isn't real."

"And this caused you to tear apart my grandfather's garage?"

"No, see," he said as he dropped into the chair opposite the desk and rested his forearms on his knees. "Um, I went to put tools away, but there were tools where my tools were supposed to go. I memorized so I wouldn't inconvenience your grandfather."

Fubar slipped off his coat and laid it on the arm of a second tattered chair in the office. Once again the muscles that had her nearly running a stop sign were tempting her as he got up to pace.

"This place is tight and small, not that I mind tight things." The smirk he gave her hoisted a dozen red flags even as he began having a bit of a meltdown of sorts. "Things need to be in place. I'm not a neat freak, far from it. Okay, maybe I am in the right context. Jesus, I know how to behave in public. Stop, Fubar, stop."

She stared at him, unsure if he was totally mental or just a little off. What had her grandfather said? He was special, slow, flicked?

"Things need to be in place. The tools are not the way Bo set them up to be. There are outlines of where he wants them, and it's a puzzle I like to solve."

"And your crew out there?"

"Underlings that must do my bidding without question," he stated and pulled in on his full lips.

"Even though you're just visiting?" While part of her was slightly interested in the inner workings of club business, another part couldn't help wondering how much longer she'd have to deal with him. Control of want wasn't high in her skill set, and the last thing her overstressed body wanted to do was be a good girl. Every deep and dirty thought in her mind was focused on how great an orgasm would be for stress release. Then her bullshit meter reminded her one-night stands were supposed to be forgotten after college.

"When your aunt from LA comes up to visit and tells you to clear the dishes, you do it, right?"

"Who said I had an aunt from LA?"

"Do you not deal in hypotheticals? They basically run my life," he said, crashing back into the chair and staring at her in a way as if he were divulging the secret of life. "The what-ifs, only I tend to actually try them instead of getting bogged down. Otherwise I'll spin out."

"Like with the tools," she offered.

"Certain things need to be in place."

"Basically you have OCD for tools?" Shelby hoped to get him calm enough to make sense of what was happening at the garage.

"Marvin said I could come back tomorrow and do this, but I would end up being up all night planning and plotting my ideas." He then shook his head as if coming back to the here and now as he stood. "Besides, I'd never have OCD, CDO sure, but never OCD."

"Never heard of it," she said trying to remember back to freshman psych and all the acronyms they had to memorize.

"It's like OCD, but in the correct order."

Shelby snickered, then stopped herself. She wasn't supposed to laugh at his foolishness.

"How long will you be?"

"Hard to tell," he admitted, then moved around the desk and sat on the edge as the back of his index finger stroked along the outside of her arm. "Am I going to be receiving any punishment for my bad behavior? I'm up for it."

"Two seconds ago you were freaking out about the misplaced tools, and now you're seeing if I'm going to pull down the screen on the door and bend you over the desk to spank you?"

"Seems like you've been thinking about it," he said. "Had a whole plan and everything. Do you get off on being dominant? I get it, but personally I have to say that I'm all about tying a woman down and—"

"And keeping her in your basement?"

"Not many basements in Cali, Vegas either," he blurted as if that fact made it impossible to pull off his devilish plan. "I said the wrong thing, didn't I?"

"Don't you always, Fubar?"

"Not with women, well, Angels mostly, I don't tend to fuck with women that aren't in the club life."

"Might be why they let you tie them down," she pointed out and started making piles of bills. "I'm not in the life, and I need to get back to my grandfather, so sorry for you losing sleep tonight, but your project will need to wait. The last thing

I need to worry about are OCD tool elves making the shop sparkly while I sleep."

"What time can I come back in the morning?" he questioned. "How early?"

"You're serious?"

"Part of the reason I was sent to Oakland is because I'm shit at lying. I know people do it, but it tends to make things worse." Her thighs actually trembled when the silvery blue of his eyes stood out under the harsh fluorescents as he took her in. "I may not tell you things, Shelby, but I'll never lie."

She considered this. How odd to not be game played by a man? Sure, he flirted, but it was bold and blatant.

"A man telling me he wants to fuck me isn't exactly groundbreaking behavior."

"Have I said I wanted to fuck you?" he asked, his brow knitting as if trying to search his memory for the moment in his OCD catalog. "I said I'd like to take you for a ride, but I can see how that would be confusing."

"You don't want to fuck me then?" she questioned as if it were an insult she couldn't accept.

"Of course I want to. You're stunning with a body I could worship for hours. But I never said it, and I don't like being accused of shit I didn't do. There's enough things I do wrong—like tonight—you can scold me for, but being an ass and saying how I'd like to fuck you until sunrise wasn't one of them."

"Do you want to fuck me until sunrise?" Jesus, the man's brutal honesty made her dizzy.

"I just said I do. Keep up, Shelby. The last thing I would have thought about you was that you were slow."

Standing and grabbing him by the shoulders, she angled

him toward the door. "Out, finish the damn garage. I'll figure something out with Pops."

"Wait, you don't want us to do this because of Bo?" he said, his hand dropping from around the door handle.

"He just had surgery." She opened the door herself only to have him slam it shut. "I can't leave you here and him alone."

"But you did that all day."

"That was different. Marvin and Tito were here." This time when she tried to open the door, he pressed harder to keep it closed.

"Marvin is still here. I'll send a Prospect to fetch Tito and have him sit in the corner to supervise."

"That's not the only reason."

"Your parameters were Marvin and Tito were working and now it's just Marvin. That's why I can't finish the work I started."

"You're infuriating." Shelby's left eye started to twitch, and she began doing the stroke checklist just in case the man was sending her over the proverbial edge.

"If I had a nickel for every time someone said that about me," he said with a shake of his head.

"Let me guess, you'd be a millionaire."

"No, not even with the synonyms for the word," he replied.

"How much then?" she challenged and watched as he drifted away for a moment.

"Forty-six dollars and eighty cents," he said when he returned to the here and now. "Did you want the total with the synonyms?"

Shelby stood fish mouthed trying to figure out if the man actually had done the math or pulled a random number out of his mind. Strangely she knew somehow it was the former. Intelligence was a turn-on, and this man fucked up beyond all recognition was more than obsessive. His hand cupped the back of her head and turned her slightly, bringing his eyes to hers, and she practically melted when he calmly spoke the words that nearly shattered her heart.

"You can't trust me, Shelby."

"You're not here visiting," she countered, swallowing to find moisture and finally catching up to the out-of-control train that was his thought process.

"No, I'm not." His other hand landed on her hip, and he cut the tiny space between them in half.

"You can't lie." The words fell breathlessly from her lips.

"I can, poorly." The pad of his thumb brushed lightly along her cheek, sending tendrils of heat along her cheek and down her neck. "Anyone with a brain can call me out on my bullshit."

"Why are you here, Fubar?"

"Call me Danny," he offered. "Or Daniel. I have no doubt the way your lips will form the sounds will send me in a tailspin."

"This your stay-silent game?"

"I'm speaking. I'm not silent." Their bodies were flush as his silvery blue eyes became heated.

"Ask me no questions, I'll tell you no lies," she murmured.

"I said I couldn't lie. I didn't say I didn't know how to keep my mouth shut." He leaned even closer. "When I touched your cheek, your eyes fluttered, but you didn't push me away. I want to kiss you, Shelby, and I've learned to read body cues that benefit me."

"Just kiss?" she countered, and her head tilted a bit when

he brushed her cheek again, sending a blaze of heat through her body.

"You know I want more than that. Let me be the bad boy phase every woman should experience at least once."

"Who says I haven't already had that phase?"

"You wouldn't look at me the way you do if you had." Stepping back, he broke the connection in a way that had her reaching back and bracing a hand on the desk for fear of tipping over. "Whoever he was didn't put to bed the want deep inside to know if it was the thrill of his no-holds-barred behavior in public or private that made women follow him."

Her ass pressed against the desk. There was an escape. It would be simple enough—he'd left her left side free even though his arm blocked the right, all so he could cradle her face with his calloused hand once more, only he didn't. Even when her head tilted slightly to the side, he allowed her space.

"Or, I'm remembering what it was like." The lie slicked her tongue with bile.

"To be with a Sinner?" he questioned, then shook his head. "The men wouldn't have been impressed by me talking with you if you'd already been through the clubhouse."

"Would that be bad?" she asked. "Being with one of your club buddies?"

The laugh that rolled from him broke the intensity that had been building. "Club buddies, that's new." He stepped back, turned, and braced himself on the desk right next to her. Even though his thigh wasn't touching hers, a part of her leg warmed. "It's adorable, like teddy bears."

"I told you I'm not in the life, and you said you only fuck women who are."

"No, I've wandered from the Angels more than once," he admitted. "Trust me, my freshman science teacher was far from a club ho."

"You slept with your freshman science teacher?" The thought disgusted her, but then again, for her, Mr. Venci had been nearing retirement and had long ago given up engaging with students. "You know that's rape."

"I do now," he acknowledged "That being said, I tend to fuck with the Angels because they don't expect much from me."

"Okay, well, this has been a dizzying conversation, and I need to make some arrangements regarding my grandfather," she said. "So please leave."

"Are you calling Tito? Or can you give me the address for my men to fetch him?"

"Tito?" she asked, trying to settle back into where that name had come from all of a sudden.

"Yes, your parameters—"

Holding her hand up, Shelby closed her eyes and did a quick but silent prayer for calm. "Go. I'm staying to supervise."

"Understood," he said, moving around her to open the door. "Um, about the other thing?"

"What other thing?" The twitching in her left eye had turned into a full-on clench, triggering a migraine.

"The fact I want to fuck you until sunrise, is that on the table for another day?" Fubar questioned as plainly as one would ask if you took sugar in your coffee. "I'm gonna be kinda busy the rest of the night."

"Out."

"That's not an answer."

"Tell me a lie," she challenged.

"You didn't ask a question. I did," he countered, and she wondered if there was any point in their interaction where she had been in charge.

Shelby shoved him through the door, slammed it closed, and rested on it to keep him from pushing back through. Slipping her phone from the hip pocket of her yoga pants, she quickly texted her cousin May. Her scolding "we need to do better" interaction from earlier had most of the cousins apologizing and offering help. May lived the closest and, as an artist, tended to be up late.

That was quick, her cousin texted. *Damn, I said I'd help but you're already needing it? Give a girl a day at least.*

Long story, Shelby texted back. *Can you or can't you? Shit at the shop needs to be addressed.*

Fine, I'll head over.

Thanks, he's asleep already from the meds.

Tucking her phone away, Shelby was comfortable enough to open the office door before she sat down at the desk. She was deep in the accounting mess and got startled when, two hours later, Fubar knocked on the open door.

four

"WOULD YOU LIKE FINAL INSPECTION?" Fubar offered, even though Marvin had already been sitting fish mouthed as if he'd never seen the garage before.

"Oh, yeah." She fumbled a bit as she tucked away a checkbook in a drawer and tapped a pile of stamped mail together to make it all uniform.

Glancing around the office, Shelby seemed a bit overwhelmed or ashamed. It was harder for him to read the difference on faces. He was doing his own inspection of the space and already felt his thumb rubbing on his middle finger. *Stop*, he scolded in his mind because the last thing he needed to do was start organizing this space. Papers weren't his thing, and this would bog him down and drown him.

"After you." Extending his hand, he ushered her through the door, taking one last look before being caught by the curve of her hip. It was hard not to when she was tugging down and smoothing the tank she wore, stealing the vision of the thin slice of her skin that peeked between the black of her pants and bright red of her top, a sliver so alluring he had to bite his bottom lip to keep from making an ass of himself again. "Stay silent, stay silent."

"What was that?" she questioned, making him aware his comment wasn't in his head this time.

"Onion rings."

She stopped one step from going into the shop, turning sharply on her heel. "Onion rings?"

"I told you I suck at lying."

"And you don't want to tell me what you said, do you?" Her brown eyes had hints of hazel in them, making it seem as if she had golden flecks. All of it allowed him to travel to a different place and not respond to her. "Right, well, let's see how your elves did."

She paused for a moment, taking in the area without so much as a candy wrapper on the floor or abandoned thermos on a tool chest.

"Open them," he said like a giddy schoolgirl, running toward the chests and pulling a drawer.

"Damn, catalogs aren't this clean," she practically gushed as her finger brushed along the shined-up tools.

"Now, I know it would mean shutting down the shop for a day or two, but I really think we should seal and paint the floor. It'll make cleanup easier." The rambling nature of him began to take over for a moment. "I mean, it's your place. All we did was clean it and put things where they belonged."

"This is more than...I can't even..." Shelby held her hand to her chest, and he worried about her reaction, until he was completely engulfed in her arms.

He slowly wrapped his arms around her, cradling the back of her neck and doing his best to not slide his other hand lower than her midback. The Prospects were standing by the doors trying not to take in the sight, causing Fubar to still, unsure how this had turned into a peep show.

"I'm sorry, it's been a long couple years with my pops, and no one has offered..." Shelby pulled back and tilted her head to the side, then waved her hand toward the other people. "Marvin, thank you also, and your buddies, friends, I don't know what to call them."

"Brothers, ma'am," Frankenstein said. "Family is good, but brotherhood bonds are different."

"Guess it only took one call to get you guys here, instead of three dozen nasty texts," she bit, swallowing back something as she turned to Fubar.

"The men have nothing but good things to say about Bo. Helping out is probably years overdue. And again, thank you for indulging my need to organize."

"Hopefully I can tap that idiosyncrasy in the future."

"You're not the first to want to tap this idiot," Rubble said, and Fubar spoke before thinking.

"Idiosyncrasy is a characteristic, not a level of intelligence."

"Guys, grab a few drinks and snacks from the store," Shelby said, quirking a bit from Fubar's response. "It's the least I could offer."

"We've snagged a few things while we were working," Fubar said. "We left our money on the counter. I figured for local and state taxes, so you should be good."

"I was offering gratis," she corrected.

There was something about being spoken to and not down

to that had his heart racing a bit. It was different than those in his past. They were placating him for an end goal. Something about Shelby told him she wasn't wanting anything from him.

"That mean we can take our money back?" Birdy questioned.

"No," Fubar said. "We don't do that shit. We inconvenienced you. Prospects, go home. She's given a seal of approval."

"Do we all get hugs?" Frankenstein asked and then slowly backed away with his hands up in surrender, as if the glare Fubar was shooting at him was laced with all sorts of *I'll fuck you up* vibes.

The sound of engines roaring soon softened as the men made their way back to the clubhouse. Moving his motorcycle back into the garage, Fubar parked it as Marvin lowered the door and checked all the locks.

"You need a ride back to your place?" Shelby asked as she stood by her SUV. "I can roll the windows down."

"No, ma'am, I'm good."

"Are you sure, Daniel?"

"I was. Now I'm not." He stumbled a bit. "I mean, it's like, what, two, maybe four, blocks, but then you said my name."

"Good night, Shelby," Marvin said as she stood awkwardly by her door.

"Night, Marv, I'll come by to check on you tomorrow." She rocked back on her heels and then forward again. "You said to call you Daniel or Danny. I can't really think of calling you Fubar seriously."

"How about ironically? Most call me it ironically," he admitted.

"I've had my bad boy. I promise I have." Her tongue flicked at her upper lip nervously. "Sorry, I don't know where that came from. I should go. You're a grown-ass man who can find his way home."

"Most days," he said. "Thank you again, you didn't have to do this. I know I can be a pain in the ass sometimes."

"If this is the way you want to hurt my ass, please do it often." Her hands covered her face as she shook her head. "That sounded so wrong."

"Kinda sounded right to me," he said. "Usually I'm not a cleaning elf, but it really would have bothered me all night, and I was hoping to do other things tonight."

"Things? Or—" She waved her hands. "Don't tell me. I don't want to know."

"Yes you do." He gave her a wink as his phone vibrated in his pants pocket, and he retrieved it to see Ice's number. While the phone wasn't preprogrammed, numbers were as vivid as faces to Fubar, and he needed no name attached to recall them. "You suck at lying too."

"Two days, Fubar, all I asked for was two days." Ice's condemning tone carried loud enough he was sure Shelby heard him.

"It was actually seventy-six hours with drive times, well over the forty-eight required for two days."

"What do you need from me?" Ice asked.

"Right now?" he said, giving Shelby a wave goodbye as he started to walk in the opposite direction. "Nothing really, I'm fine in Oakland for a few days, weeks, I don't know how long, but they can stand me, so that's something."

"I put feelers out, and Grimm said as of right now, the guy

isn't even missed by Brambilla. Here's hoping you can come home soon."

Fubar glanced back at the taillights of Shelby's car as it turned right, disappearing from sight.

"What happened?" Ice asked. "Do you even remember?"

"Not really." He ran his fingers through his hair and shook off the night filled with sickly satisfying projects. "Came out of it with a dead guy between my legs. You know, how Bree feels now that you're practically married."

"Your jokes are weaker than reheated three-day-old coffee."

"Again, like Bree feels—"

"Why are you my friend again?" Ice said with a hardy laugh behind his words.

"Poor life choices," Fubar said, quoting his father twice in the same day. "Fucked up my bike pretty bad. Been fixing it up at that corner mechanic's place."

"You've been fixing it up? Not the mechanic?"

"He had surgery, and I'm bored."

"Yeah, that's probably a good idea then," Ice acquiesced. "Are you sure you're okay there? I can get you the route to Seattle, or—"

"No, I like Oakland. King's cool. You remember my buddy Toad. He's here, and Calix had me practically pissing myself earlier."

"Hey, Fubar, we need you!" Ace hollered once Fubar stepped into the clubhouse.

"Call me if you hear any change," he said before slipping his phone into his back pocket again.

"Where's your cut?" Ace asked, and Fubar glanced over his shoulder, instantly remembering he'd taken it off in the office.

"Fuck," he spat, shocked he'd been so distracted by Shelby and the cleanup he'd left it behind.

"Yeah, well, I'll have someone else kick your ass later for that infraction. I need an Enforcer to handle a pair of bitch-ass thieves that took some product off one of our street boys."

"Guess I'm low man on the totem," he reasoned. "Sure, you got them caught, or do I have to hunt and chase?"

"We know where they are. I was going in, just needed back-up," Ace said. "Grab a hoodie, and let's go."

"On it." Fubar rushed to the room he was crashing in and pulled a dark hoodie over his head. The weapon of choice, a simple Glock on his hip, even though he rarely used the damn thing. Fists were much more satisfying.

Less than five minutes from stepping into the clubhouse and Fubar was back out the door and driving a van as he followed Ace, Frankenstein, and Nitro. The low-rent apartment building showed signs of being a Section 8 flop with good paperwork that kept the inspectors away.

"27 B," Ace said, and Fubar didn't wait for instructions.

The trigger had been flipped, and he barreled full speed into the building marked B with a broken security door.

"Shit, man, wait up," one of the men called, but they didn't understand how an order was given, location assigned, and he was the man who ran. Exhaustion wouldn't hit him for hours yet, but all a good fight could do would bring it on sooner. Like a kid who swam all day, a few good knocks to the opponent's head, and he would be ready for his head to meet the pillow.

Acid burned through his veins as he took in the number pattern and soon realized he'd have to be on the second floor. Taking the steps two by two in the stairwell, he only had to go past one door before he was in front of 27 B. He drew his weapon, stomped his foot on the door handle, and sent the knob bouncing down the hallway as he entered. Sweeping the space with his gun, he caught sight of their product spread out on a table. A man stood up holding his own weapon, and Fubar shot, aiming for the shoulder. The man fell back and to the right with a howl, bringing a second from the bedroom, and Fubar used the butt of his gun to throat punch him.

The injured man shot wildly around the apartment, and Fubar swung the extra man in front of him like a shield, counting the blasts to calculate when he could drop the dead barrier. Dog walking the body toward his roommate, hoping he knew the clip well enough, he was pretty sure it was empty now as he tossed one man on top of the other.

The first howled, not in pain, but disgust and realization that his friend was dead by his own hand. "What the fuck, Johnny? Come on, man."

"I'd say, 'Tell your friends,' but I assume he's your only one," Fubar said as the rest of the Sinners rolled into the melee. "Don't fuck with Sinners or Sinner-adjacent personnel. Collect the product, Frankenstein."

"You fucking killed him," Nitro said.

"No, I didn't," Fubar said matter-of-factly. "The guy blubbering over there did."

Once in the hall, Ace slammed Fubar against the wall. "What the fuck! We were going to talk to them and maybe rough them up. That's it."

"You gotta be clear about that kinda shit."

"Clear? I said you were backup."

"Oh, fuck, you did. That's my bad," he said, making his way

back out of the building with the men double-timing behind him.

"That's your bad? That's your bad! Fubar, what if I had the wrong apartment?"

Fubar stopped walking, smacked Frankenstein in the chest, and held his hand out. "Give me a baggie."

He did, and Fubar shook it in front of Ace's face. "I know this pretty mug at fifty paces," he said of the skull they used to mark product. "Here's the deal. You give me an order, and I execute. I like having a few friends along, but don't need them. Think of me as a pit bull that simply needs a command, nothing more."

"They put pits down for being too aggressive."

"And they might do that to me one day. Until then, *woof woof*."

five

A COUSIN VIDEO chat meeting had Shelby anxious, not for the subject matter, but because if Pops overheard, there would be hell to pay. No one wanted to be a burden on their family. They wanted to have people come over because they were loved, not required to.

"Look, it's simple. We need to take turns looking out for Pops," she said. "Those that are out of town need to plan a vacation. We don't know how much longer we'll have him."

"You have been carrying most of the load, but don't act like you haven't benefited from it," Patrick, one of the older and chronically on-a-hustle cousins, said. "You lost your big-time corporate job and fell right into one at the shop."

"I didn't lose it, I stepped away, and running the shop ain't exactly paying my bills. Maybe if Pops had family around, he'd see the point of retiring and selling the business."

"And who would that benefit?" Patrick accused as suddenly every box on her screen was paying attention.

"He would. It would go in his retirement," she snapped. "I don't want him to quit the garage to make some come up. I want him to quit so he can rest his back and enjoy a sunset without the smell of forty weight oil wafting through the garage."

Everything couldn't be about money. Sure, they had different parents, but at least her siblings should be on board with her idea and not thinking she was just after money. The last thing she cared about was how much she'd get after Pops died. The best part of her life had been in that place, her grandmother and her, and now Pops with his jokes and grumbles, the quiet way he was teaching her basic maintenance but not shoving it down her throat.

"If it wasn't for Shelby, he'd probably be blind as a bat and getting sued for putting the wrong part in a car," May said, finally giving her an ally. "The other night she was supervising work at the garage, and I was at home with Pops. It's a mess, and not like a hoarder, but more like someone who has given up on doing more than the minimum."

"That's on me too," Shelby admitted. "I had no problem working at the shop, but I didn't take him up on offers for dinner after work. These are little moments that mean so much to him, you have no idea. I get it, Nana kept us together, but we are disrespecting her by not keeping it up."

"I'll make up a schedule," Alicia said. The first grandchild, she should have been the one to take this on, but she'd moved to Colorado a decade ago. "And get a shared doc going. Everyone has until the end of the week to sign up for their time. End of story. I'll set up to come out to San Fran for a week or so with the kids."

"Thank you, Alicia," Shelby said, feeling a bit of weight lifting off her shoulders. "Pops is up. I'm going to make him a quick breakfast before we go to work. He's demanding to get out of the house today."

"Baby steps with him," Henry said. "Remember what Nana used to say."

A chorus of cousins repeated her warning: "Bo could start an argument in an empty house."

Whipping up some oatmeal, Shelby diced up some strawberries and dropped a few blueberries in the mix.

"I like brown sugar and cinnamon," he grumbled.

"Blueberries are good for your eyes," she pointed out and placed the bowl in front of him.

"Didn't insurance just pay to fix my eyes?"

"Let's keep them that way." She sat across from him with her own bowl.

"When are you going back to your apartment?"

"My winning personality not what you expected?"

"You have a life, don't you?" he said. "You should be getting married and starting a family."

"Where is this nonsense coming from?"

"Why is that biker still hanging around the shop? Marvin said he's been there every day." Pops ate a few bites of the oatmeal and gave a reluctant smile of approval. "His bike's been done."

"Maybe he wants your approval. Wasn't that the deal you struck?"

"Maybe he wants my blessing," Pops said, not giving an inch. "I remember looking at a girl once the way he's looking at you."

"How is he looking at me?" she countered, not about to have a sex talk with her grandfather.

"The same way you seem to be drooling over him."

"Pops!" He wasn't lying, but she'd tried to be better about staring. She'd tried, but just because the son of a bitch may be a little weird didn't mean he wasn't funny, smart, and knew how to drive a woman crazy. "Okay, now that we're out of fantasyland, can we get to the shop? You wanted to go in today."

"Your nana used to make her brother come along so I behaved. Am I being a chaperone? I don't mind it, but I thought you might find it old-fashioned."

Narrowing her eyes at him, Shelby shook her head. "There is nothing between me and Daniel."

"Oh, Daniel, I'm pretty sure that's not what the other men call him."

"It's his given name, and I don't care what others call him. I call him Daniel." After gathering the dishes, she finished getting ready, and they made their way to the shop.

Even with his oversized sunglasses protecting his eyes, her grandfather instantly started fussing with things outside. Around the gas pumps he saw trash, but when he finally made it into the shop, he stood gobsmacked at the cleaned place. He wandered from one tool chest to another as Marvin tapped Fubar, who was pouring oil into his engine.

"Hey Bo, Shelby said it would be okay for us to do a little organizing."

"Hell, I thought the docs put rose-colored lenses in these glasses, this place is so clean." Rubbing his chin a bit, Pops sat on one of the shop stools and took in the organized shop. "Guess I let a few things go over the last few years."

"It's your place. You can let anything you want go," Fubar said.

"So glad I got your permission. Shelby, you hear that? This guy says I can let things go."

"Yeah, could mean you could sell it too." She beamed.

* * *

When Shelby returned to the shop, it was under protest if the way she chased after Bo was any determination. There was a way her nose would crinkle when she was upset that set off small brush fires on Fubar's skin.

"Pops, I swear if you even try to push that toolbox one inch, I will find a way to beat you for old and new," Shelby spat.

"Child, don't try to use my words against me," he countered, then slipped into pure innocence. "I was just trying to get to the plug behind the chest."

"I've got you." Fubar popped up from where he was reassembling his motor. After wiping his hands on a rag, he took the charger, but when he moved the tool chest, there wasn't a plug to be had. "Um, there isn't—"

"I know what isn't there, boy," Bo barked. "I just wanted the damn chest put where it belongs."

"Then where is that?" he asked. "I'll move it."

Bo's lips pursed, and Fubar was sure, on the other side of the dark plastic sunglasses he was forced to wear, his eyes were narrowing. "I'm not infirmed."

"I can tell, but a few weeks without lifting won't kill you. Plus, it'll make it so you can see nests in motors from fifty paces."

Bo's arthritic finger pointed about five feet from where the chest was sitting. It made sense because the access was more convenient.

"Aren't you supposed to be fixing your bike, not playing Alice from *The Brady Bunch* and tidying up?"

"It's easier when I know where the tools I need are."

Bo grumbled a bit and made his way over to Fubar's bike. "Now look here." His foot toed at the pile of screws, washers, and bolts, making them scatter a bit, and Fubar clenched his fist for a moment before dropping down to a knee to straighten them back out.

"Pops, if you're going to be a problem and not the solution, I will take you home," Shelby snapped as she knelt by Fubar and helped put them back in order.

"It's fine," he said. "Trust me, I've had worse."

"He feels useless and wants to take it out on all of us," she explained, and he stilled when her finger accidentally brushed his. "I thought coming and seeing the shop running fine would help him stop fussing around the house. Now he's just fussing here."

"He's the boss, right?" Fubar asked, then stood to face the older man. "I know how to follow directions. If you tell me how to do it right, I'll be your hands, and you'll have fixed my bike."

Bo narrowed his eyes a bit, then gave three directions in rapid-fire mode. A test, one Fubar had known how to pass from age three. Directions were easy, but part of him was cataloging the orders for future use. The man had a few decades of knowledge he wanted to absorb, and once they got past Bo feeling useless, he turned into a teacher. A damn good one that had Fubar's ass sitting at the front of the class.

Three hours later his bike roared to life once again, sounding better than when it rolled off the lot. He could see Bo's eyes drooping a bit, but not from the swelling or bright lights that had him fighting with his glasses all day. This was from exhaustion as he disappeared into the office.

A few minutes later, Shelby's hand was stroking the leather seat of his bike. "Thank you for that. If I could get him home, I'm sure he'd sleep till dawn."

"Then take him."

"You've met him, right? He's a bit stubborn and itches to find ways to fight," she pointed out.

"Nah." Fubar turned the engine off and couldn't take his eyes from her fingertips stroking the leather. "He likes things done right and knows way too many people who do them wrong. I've never had a better teacher."

She turned, resting her ass sideways on his seat. If she were a man, that would be a call to arms. Then again, he'd been known to push, with a bit of force, more than one woman from his bike's seat. Only he wanted her to stay, spread her legs just enough that he could fit in between, and let her hands rest on his hips, his own being a bit too busy exploring her curves. Did she know what she was doing? Or was this just Shelby being Shelby? Club women majored in cock teasing only to get him annoyed, not turned on.

"Pops has wanted a student for decades." Her right index finger traced the metal Harley emblem on the fuel tank.

"You prefer retail sales to turning a wrench?"

"I'm a girl."

"I've noticed," he said, taking her comment as an invitation and stepping close. The soft curve of her lips danced in his mind, and he wondered if it would be safe to kiss her. Part of him called out to throw caution to the wind, take the chance, but he stopped a bit too close as he tried to speak and could feel himself stumbling over words. "You respect the trade, don't you?"

"Yes, as did my father, but he demanded that I go to college like his father did. If Pops really wanted one of us to take over the family business, he probably shouldn't have pushed so hard for us to get four-year degrees."

"When a two-year one would have worked," Fubar said, knowing he had to get away from her, only to be drawn in closer. "Were you drinking fruit punch?"

"Um? What?" Her eyes wrinkled at the edges as she stood and moved from his bike back into the garage.

"Your lips, they are bright red, but not like a lipstick."

Her fingers instantly covered her lips as if they could tell the color, or maybe it was shame.

"I found a stash of cherry Dum-Dum suckers," she admitted, then went to his bike again, this time leaning over to inspect her lips in one of his side mirrors. "Oh my goodness, those are red."

"Do they still taste like cherries?" He came up behind her and brought a hand to rest on her hip. She jolted up and spun on her heel to face him with a quick cut of her eyes down to her hip, just one, his hand having never left her body when she spun around.

"Daniel." Her tone confused him more than most did. Then again, her look was what made him pause and step back. Not because she appeared angry with him, but he wasn't sure she wanted him to touch her. Best to rule on the side of caution.

69

"I'm sorry, I didn't mean to..." Tucking his head, he turned, only to have her capture his hand to stop him. "Shelby, it's probably best if you don't."

"Don't what?" she asked, her soft fingers wrapping around his rough ones. "You really wanted to know if the flavor lingered, didn't you?"

He nodded, keeping his eyes on the blacktop of the driveway. "Contrary to popular belief, I'm not some sweet-talking man."

"You're honest and blunt." Her other hand reached up, catching his chin and turning it so he was looking at her.

"*Simple* is the word most think of when talking about me."

"The last thing you are, Daniel, is simple."

His thumb stroked along his middle finger, trying to still his brain from running a thousand miles an hour into a brick wall. It was there, right in front of him, calling him Daniel and not the fuckup everyone else did, with gold-flecked brown eyes, soft lashes, and a softer heart.

"I can't flirt, Shelby, but you make me want to try," he said. "I don't know how to be that person, even though I want to know why flicking a few drops of water on a girl is supposed to make them get out of their clothes."

"Because they're wet." She tilted her head a bit and gave him a sweet smile.

"Barely, a few spots that will dry in a matter of minutes on a normal day."

"That's part of the joke. The foolishness of it all."

"I can't be that person for you, or anyone."

"I never asked you to," she said as her grandfather came out and called for her to bring him home. "Coming, Pops."

When Shelby moved away from him, his body cooled, and he sat to the side on his bike, watching her load Bo into her car.

"Hey Daniel," she called, her smile brightening the already warm day, and he acknowledged her with a nod. "I like that I make you want to try."

"Enough to see the sunrise with me?" he asked, hoping she understood without him having to verbalize out loud in front of everyone the whole "fuck until sunrise" offer he made.

"Not today."

"That's not a no," he called out as she got into her SUV and drove away. "It's not a no."

"What's not a no?" Tito asked.

"Hot Cheetos."

"Hot Cheetos," Tito said, nodding his head like Fubar was a moron.

His opinion didn't change the fact that Shelby didn't think he was simple. More importantly, she hadn't said no.

six

FUBAR HAD to get away with 90 percent of his shit based on looks alone. Shelby had begun to envy him over the last few weeks, the forgiveness given to the beautiful in the world mixed with how easily he learned new tasks with his photographic memory of all things related to his past. But that wasn't what made him intelligent. Even a monkey could repeat a process to perfection. Having the ability to determine the need and work out the details was another thing. How could she hate, envy, and lust over a man all at the same time?

The shop needed a third mechanic, and even Pops had to admit it was nice to have a break from the hard part of being one. Giving Fubar instructions gave him a set of eyes, hands, and muscles that allowed for jobs to be finished. It was almost like having a robot he could program without using a keypad. The man was an Alexa—*do this, do that*—without so much as clarification. And he knew all the parts, allowing him to give feedback on repair needs.

It didn't hurt that the man was eye candy for her and the new increase of female traffic to the area. An alert must have gone out with how many more people were getting their gas, snacks, and tobacco products from the Fill-Up and Fix-Up. She had to call in their vendor early to restock shelves. Those were the good ones, the ones she didn't have a pang of jealousy with, unlike the ones who wandered in as if the corner mechanic was a new pop-up business they'd never heard of before.

"Hey Shel," Fubar said, making one lookie-loo stop her fake dilemma over corn chips or cheese popcorn when he wandered into the store from the shop. "We're going to need to order a fan belt for that Chevy in there, and Pops said he's almost out of fifty weight oil, so he wanted you to call up the guy to refill the barrel."

"Already?" she questioned as the woman with the bodycon dress gave up on the salty and plucked a Blow Pop from the plastic jug at the register.

"I'll just take a couple of these," she practically purred, not looking at Shelby as she locked down on Fubar. "I think I need to suck on something for a bit."

"One fifty," she snapped as the woman tossed some quarters on the counter.

"You're short one," Fubar said without a hint of malice. "Shel said one fifty. You only have five quarters."

"Aren't you observant?" The customer took off the white wrapper and rolled the pink candy on her tongue before pulling in hard, then popping it out. "Anything else about me got your attention?"

"Not really," he said. "You got that other quarter? If not, take two back and put the second sucker in the jar."

Funny how Fubar said he didn't get subtle hints. He wasn't the only one. This woman couldn't get a full-on hint that he didn't give a shit about her shitty game of seduction.

"Oh, I got a quarter. I've got a lot of everything."

"You'll probably need antibiotics then," he said as he tapped the counter, and the woman fished another quarter from her purse before storming out. "I said something wrong, didn't I?"

"She wanted to suck your dick. Did you not get that?"

"Huh? She probably should have said, *I want to suck your dick*, or *cock* or *penis* even," he reasoned. "I get it, the sucker thing. I mean, how hard is it to just say what you want? I'm open to pretty much anything if asked. It wouldn't be the first time someone said, *Hey, let me suck your dick*. Who turns that down?"

"That how your science teacher phrased it?"

"Mrs. Eskar? No. Well, one time after she got to know me better, but it was more like a confession. *I want to feel every part of you.* I agreed. I wanted to feel every part of her. So we locked the door and—"

"Don't want to know. Again, it was rape. You were what? Fourteen? Fifteen?"

"Yeah, both of those years, a little when I was sixteen, then her husband wanted a kid."

"And you saw nothing wrong with sleeping with a married woman?"

"I wasn't married. I wasn't doing anything wrong," he countered with a logic she had to respect. "I've never made a commitment for even monogamy with a woman."

"Fubar—Daniel—you confound me on the best days and fluster me on the worst."

"That tracks," he said, leaning in close with a half smirk, making her want to bite on his lips. "You want to know my feelings toward you?"

Fuck yes she did. If nothing else, the man was blunt when truthful. Only he'd said something that stopped her from nodding. He'd never been a boyfriend to anyone? How was that? No one tried to lock his ass down? The crimson flag waved high on that one, but then again, when he spun out or got in one of his loops of logic, it could be dizzying in a bad way.

"I'm afraid to know," she stated. "And honestly, my heart can't take the life you offer."

"Being a biker who randomly comes home with cut knuckles and black eyes?"

"No." She shook her head. "Strangely, that I could live with."

"Then what?" he asked as one of their regulars came in for his oil change and rotation appointment.

"Later, maybe," she said, pulling up the man's records as Fubar slipped back into the shop.

Passing the customer off to Tito, Shelby pulled up the specs for the fan belt, then called their distributor and set up a delivery for the next day on the oil. Then she picked up her phone for the cousin group chat. She needed a break from Pops and the shop completely.

Who remembers how to run the register, I need a day or two off.

The call for help went out, and she printed off an inventory sheet. Not surprisingly it took a few hours before anyone responded. She'd prodded a few times with some gentle texts: *The pay is shit, but I'll put you on payroll. Pops will let you run the air compressor. Don't make me call your parents.*

The last one triggered a response from her cousin Quinton. He never wanted Aunt Ruth called, let alone Uncle Byron. Those two had a one-two punch to keep all three of their kids in line. Quinton, being the oldest, wasn't going to put up with punishment when it could be avoided.

"That was low, Shelby," he said when she answered his call. "I have a job, you know. I can't just take off."

"You have PTO? Because if you have PTO or sick leave, you can. Cough, say you puked up what you assume is your liver, I don't care. I've worked six days a week for the last few years here. I need more than Sundays off."

"Damn, Cuz, alright. I'll make it work. What's got your panties in such a twist?"

"Nothing, Q, I just want a break from the smell of old oil and sweat," she lied. Shelby needed distance from Fubar before she walked up to him and said she wanted to be fucked until sunrise. It was right there on the tip of her tongue, and she had a feeling he'd be more than happy to oblige. What man would turn that down?

"You want me tomorrow, or can I take Monday and Tuesday for you?"

"Two days? Two days, I'll work tomorrow if I can have you here on Monday and Tuesday. You're my hero."

"I'll do it on one condition," he said. "You can't spend the time cleaning Pops' place. I've been organizing the rest of us to do a top-to-bottom cleaning."

"You're not my hero, you're my God. I'm going to end up worshiping you in ways that are blasphemous."

Fubar walked in on the second half of her conversation as he went to the cooler and removed a water.

"Q, I have to go, customers," she lied again and saw the arch in Fubar's eyebrow judging her a bit.

"What about my life hurts your heart?" he questioned as he twisted the top off the bottle of water, then chugged the whole thing at once. She marveled at the way his mouth surrounded the opening and how the muscles along his neck worked. It was wrong. She was as bad as the Blow Pop girl with her ogling of the man.

"Don't worry about it," she offered, and he walked over and flipped the sign to *Closed*. It was that time of day, but this seemed different, the way he did it as he spun the lock on the door. He was trapping her in with him, and when she scanned the shop, she saw even her grandfather was gone and the bays all closed. "What's going on?"

"What about my life would hurt your heart?" He stepped behind the counter, and she was officially trapped by the body she desperately wanted to be under, over, and in a myriad of positions, both legal and illegal, with.

"Other women." Her comment was empty, and it was fucked up that she'd made it knowing how he would take it.

"What other women?"

"The ones who come up and say, *I want to suck your dick*," she said. "The fact that you have a group of women who fuck on command at your fingertips."

"Have you ever fucked on command?" he asked, his hands

locking on the counter on either side of her. "Or have men played games to seduce you into their beds? There's a freedom that comes with being open and honest with your wants and desires."

"You can't lie to me, right?"

"I can lie to anyone, but I highly doubt you'd believe me," he countered.

"How many woman have you been with since you came to Oakland?"

"Been with?" he questioned. "Or fucked? Use your words to get an accurate answer, Shelby."

"Fucked, in any form."

"None." There was no joking, bad pun, or random word that made no sense in his response. "First night I was tired, then I met you. That's probably the reason. The only time I even think about sex is when you're around me. I'm sure a shrink would say that's why I'm at the shop as much as I am."

"Bullshit." Her heart clenched because she knew it wasn't a lie or a game he was playing. Fubar didn't seduce, and yet his words had her practically panting as he reached over and flipped the outside lights off, officially closing the shop.

"You never let me take you for a ride," he said. "My bike's been working for over a week. Go for a ride with me."

She wasn't sure if it was an order or an offer. Either way, the more she was around him, she found it harder to refuse his requests. Simple, complex, all of them were completed without question. Then again, all of them were direct.

"All you want is to take me for a ride on your bike?" she asked.

"I thought we established I want to fuck you until sunrise."

"And that's the problem," she said, ducking under his arms

only to have him turn around and catch her at her waist. Heat erupted along her back when it was pressed to his front. Her mind swam as he tucked back her spiral curls and brushed his lips along the column of her neck. "I want the next sunset, and the one after that, and the one after that. I'm not looking for one night, Daniel. We're both grown, and grown people want more than a night to remember. They want a lifetime of them."

"Like your grandparents had?" he surmised. "But no one knows going in what a relationship will be."

"You've never had a relationship," she rebutted.

"That's because no one wanted more than a few stolen moments with me," he confessed, his arms loosening around her belly, and she locked her hand around his wrist. "What did you say again? I confound and frustrate you? Even those who were supposed to be in my life forever walked away. It's not that I never wanted to be with a woman for more than an orgasm. They never wanted that from me."

"Maybe I like handfuls." Turning in his arms, she snaked her arms around his back.

"I have a feeling you would really enjoy sex with me then," he said, and she shook her head at him.

"Was that your attempt at a joke? Or was it a lie?"

"I can't lie to you, Shelby," he said. "But I can boast truths."

"You're going back to Vegas." The statement was hard and gut-wrenching because she couldn't leave her grandfather, not now. After all she'd seen from his home, it wasn't feasible.

"I don't have to. I can transfer chapters. I love my brothers there, but if I could make a life beyond the club, they would be happy. Lord knows I have little more than an apartment there."

"Are you saying I could be more than a fuck?" she asked.

"You've always been." He cradled her face in his hands and leaned down.

His lips, gentle at first, became hungered as his tongue delved into her mouth. Curling her fingers, she clung to the jumpsuit he wore when working to protect his clothes. The two of them got lost in the moment. His hands slid down her arms to her hips, and he lifted her off the ground to set her on the counter. Her legs locked around his waist, and she couldn't help busting the snaps of his jumpsuit. Finally her fingers were able to go under his tank and run over his taut abdomen. His lips trailed down her neck and found the crook at her shoulder, setting her off.

In one swift movement, her shirt was over her head and tossed to the side as he brought his mouth to her bra and bit the cotton over her nipple. The *ting-ting* sound of tires running over the alert rope at the pumps had her pushing him back—to stop not only him, but herself.

"Not here," she breathed, recognizing cameras were running and there was a 90 percent chance someone would be at the door knocking to get her to turn on the pumps in less than a minute.

"Go for a ride on my bike," he said, and she nodded, hopping off the counter and running to find her shirt.

Her back was turned when a knock came on the door, and as she slipped her shirt over her torso, she looked back to see Fubar pointing to the *Closed* sign. A set of praying hands had him flipping on the pump and letting the person fuel up before they fully shut down the shop.

After stepping out of his coveralls, he adjusted his boots and slung his leather coat on as the chorus of "Sex and Candy" played for her and her alone in her mind. When they finished locking up, he passed her a helmet, and she held it close to her chest.

"What's going to happen?" she questioned as if a ride on a bike would be the end of the world she knew.

He turned over the engine and scooted forward to make room for her on the back.

"I've only got plans until sunrise. After that, I'll let you be in charge."

* * *

There were few academic aspects of life Fubar couldn't master with the right motivation. For the most part, it was the slowness of the teacher that bored him and had him moving on because the end prize wasn't worth his effort. Shelby was worth a lifetime of study. She understood his eccentricities. The fact he responded differently in social settings, which made him a joke to most, she could grasp. He wasn't a smart-ass or sarcastic. He was blunt and honest in a way the normal people were only recently coming to grips with.

His father was in the generation scoffing at the words *autistic, attention deficit hyperactivity disorder, bipolar, OCD, sensory processing, anxiety*. All of it was a sign of weakness and needing to take a switch to the boy to get it worked out of him. That had been the way his father was raised, and in many ways, it did set him to rights. Having researched the diagnoses he should have been given as a child, he started to understand the ones missed in his father. Perhaps the issues were more severe in Fubar's case, because you couldn't smack the OCD from him. In fact, it heightened the need to fix the unsettled, to avoid the pain.

"You have to wear the helmet," he snapped when Shelby didn't immediately put it on. Her hair wasn't constrained by a bun that would have made the helmet hard to wear. Instead it was loose and perfect for him to twist a finger around the tight spirals.

"I can't stay with you until sunrise," she replied meekly as her fingers drummed unevenly on the visor of his helmet. "Pops is still under weight restrictions."

"May is with him. She came by while we were finishing the tire rotation to take him to a concert in the park," he said. "Didn't you see her come by? Where did you think your granddad went?"

"I thought he walked home. He was having a good day." She shook her head. "He's been so good this week I started to fall back into the old ways."

"Not fully," Fubar reasoned. "Unless you don't want to go with me. I can't assuage your fears or promise a heart won't be harmed. Although I'm far from a sociopath, I don't fully grasp the emotion of love. Though if you ask any of the men I call brother if I am loyal and true, know that I am. For them I would kill without a second thought if asked. You are no different in my mind."

"No different than King or Toad or Calix?"

"There are a few differences," he said, reaching out and tugging her to his side as he straddled the bike.

One hand drifted down to her ass, while the other slid under her hair to cradle her head. Soft curls tickled his palm as he brought her lips to his. Touch, sensation, all of it was different for him, and he knew this. He needed a certain thread count on his bed, or the sheets would be scratchy. Different lotions on a woman's skin would make her smooth to most, but sticky to him. Shelby had a lip gloss with a hint of blackberries and a silken quality, making their embrace one he didn't want to break.

His tongue met hers as they deepened the kiss and her fingers tangled in his hair, a tug sending blood rushing down his body. With her, there was no thought to his attraction. It was automatic. He didn't have to prep or command his dick to swell. One glance with a curve of her lips had his length hardening to the point of pain. Grasping the globe of her ass sent him over the moon. Emotions, hormone-rushing needs were things he'd tamped down and controlled because for most there was no difference in the rush. Not with Shelby. He wanted to experience every sense because it was intense and consuming.

"Put on the helmet." His order was rarely denied by others, civilian or in the life, and Shelby would not be the first. He dipped his shoulder, and her hand used him for leverage as she mounted the bike and located the back foot pedals. When her arms wrapped around his waist, he inhaled slowly to take in the moment. To remember how the world had been when his life truly started. For now that he had her, he wasn't going to let the woman go.

There was one thing California had plenty of, beach. It didn't take long to find a place where he could tuck away his bike. After grabbing a few items from his saddlebags, he walked her down a rough but passable path to where he'd already set up a driftwood teepee fire pit.

"Just found a random place?" she questioned as he lit the fire after spreading out a king-size comforter.

"I don't sleep much in general," he said. "Used to drive my dad crazy when I was younger."

"Your dad still around?"

"He's alive and policing the streets of Las Vegas, if that's what you mean." Pops and snaps came from the dry wood as fire began darkening it.

"But aren't the Sinners outlaws?" She sat, smoothing out the blanket, then toed off her tennis shoes and set them on the edge. "I mean, you're all good with us, but don't you do bad things?"

"Everyone does bad things," he countered as he tugged on the laces of his boots. "Some within the law, some outside it."

Taking off his cut, he was sure to give it the reverence needed and hung it on a branch from a tree that had fought its way through the hard rock wall.

"Take this tree. Every law says it shouldn't be here because rock is mightier than wood, and yet, here it is. Should we punish it for being able to overcome a law it doesn't agree with?"

"Is that your justification for doing bad things?" she questioned when he lay back and she curled into his arms. Her leg locked around his as the stars began pinpricking the black velvet of night.

"Thought you already had your bad boy," he challenged. "I remember you saying that. Are you trying to get out of this before it starts?"

"What are you planning on starting?"

The pad of his middle finger trailed down her shoulder to

the exposed skin at her elbow. The shift from cotton to flesh had fire burning through his palm.

"First, a little kissing, followed by me stripping off your shirt, then bra, as you straddle me. I'll suckle each of your nipples for an appropriate amount of time. Then you and I will either roll over and I continue to strip you down, following the clothing with my mouth, or you'll stay on top and you'll ride me naked until you come so loud your scream will echo up the wall and only the crashing waves will be able to drown it out."

"On anyone else that would be boasting," she countered.

"But you know I don't have the capacity to be hyperbolic."

"I'm not having sex on the beach with you."

"Why? Don't like the drink?"

"I thought you couldn't joke?" she said, smacking his chest.

"I've learned about dual meanings and used them to my advantage." It was nothing for him to snatch her by the waist and shift her so her knees were bent on either side of his hips. "I've driven by this place three times in the last few days, and no one comes here."

"You sure?"

"Do you really care?" he asked, sliding his hand under her shirt, splaying his fingers as her belly trembled against his palm. "I'm pretty sure I could make you not care."

"Boastful."

He stripped off her shirt and cupped her breasts, running his thumb over the soft fabric of her bra until her nipple began pebbling.

"Daniel," she warned, until he pulled her mouth to his.

The request to stop was lost as her hips began grinding on his length and the two of them came together. Waves crashed on the rocky shore as heat licked them from the small bonfire when the wind blew off the Pacific. His fingers made light work of her bra, and he trailed a mix of kisses and licks until he was able to bring one breast into his mouth. Her short fingernails raked along the back of his head and down his neck as the first moan escaped when he flicked the hard peak of her nipple.

Blacking out was different when it came with sex rather than fighting. The loss of control was the same. He became an animal with very little ability to rein himself in, only he remembered every second. Drawn out and in slow motion, he turned her over and pulled off her jeans. The moon was nearly full as she became bathed in its light, a vision he would treasure until his dying day. He shimmied her panties down and brought her ankle to his shoulder once the fabric had cleared her flesh.

Darkened skin met his lips as he moved back up to her thighs. The glistening of her wanton sex called to him, and he buried himself between her sweet folds. Her body met his mouth as she locked the leg from his shoulder around the back of his neck. Undulating hips rolled as he flicked her clit with his tongue before thrusting inside to taste her fully, the sweetness coating it and trickling down his throat as he gripped her thigh tight.

It was a coin flip on who was holding on tighter, him for fear of losing himself or her for fear of letting him go before the orgasm rocked through her body. Of all his studies, discovering how to locate the G-spot on any woman was his favorite. He never understood how men could say it didn't exist or the female orgasm was a myth. A bundle of tightly wound nerves inside and connected to the clit. The simplicity of knowing where the clit was and curling a finger to find the back of it was all it took.

He loved suckling and teasing the orgasm out of a woman, especially when she'd never had the full experience—a man who not only gave it to them, but didn't let it stop. Her slick channel welcomed his fingers as he curled them upward and found the tight bundle. With one finger on each side, he began to wobble them as he increased the suction on her clit.

"Oh my God," she screamed above him, her body shifting from side to side as if trying to get away, only he wouldn't let her.

This was his specialty, the thing he treasured most in life, because unlike with his dick, he was completely in control. The pace, the length, and knowing the exact location as her wetness moved from thin to thick. Her scream echoed off the walls as he'd predicted as she practically bent in two and balanced on the crown of her head. The convulsions around his fingers as her flavor shifted from sweet berries to salted toffee told the one thing he never misread. Faces could be deceitful, words could be a lie, but a woman's body going through an actual orgasm where flavor and touch were involved could not be denied. There was no "Katz's Deli from *When Harry Met Sally*" display of pleasure confusing a person with howls and faces twisting to prove a point.

Shelby rode the orgasm as it crested and crashed her back to earth. She'd tried to crawl away as if unworthy of pleasure when her thighs began trembling on either side of his head, her body taut until the experience burst forth. He slowly removed his fingers to allow a moment of rest as he sheathed his length in a condom from his pocket. He watched as her body twisted and turned on the blanket as if he no longer existed above her.

The bend of her knees was bringing a point to her toes as her hips hovered, waiting for his hand to slide beneath her. He could have stayed stroking his dick from this visual and been completely satisfied, but she wouldn't have been, and that would never do.

seven

SHELBY WASN'T sure if leaving her body was possible, but there was no room for her brain with every nerve on fire. It had checked out completely and was hanging on the beach, waiting for her to return to the land of the living. There was no chance she'd come that hard and that fast, but when Fubar thrust inside her, stretching her, but not in a painful way, every muscle in her body seized. There was no chance since the only resistance her body could produce was from the clenching of her core. He didn't pull back more than an inch before slamming inside her over and over. Was it the ocean or her own blood rushing in her ears drowning out the world around them? The man had stripped her naked on the beach when she rarely took off a cover-up there.

Her inhibitions were gone when she was in his arms. There was a safety when he was around that had her arms holding tight as he pounded inside and sent her reeling, the weight of him not crushing, with the scent of man mixed with oil and leather. Fresh ocean spray misted in the air with each crash of the waves, and when he was as deep inside her as he could be, he rolled the two of them until she was on top of him. With her knees bent on either side of him, he hit a spot of her she didn't know existed.

Glancing down at him, she saw the icy eyes that transfixed her on a good day were practically glowing from the moonlight. His hand was spread across her belly as she rocked on his dick and balanced her hands on his chest. When had he taken off his tank top? It had to be when she was lost in the feel of him hitting her abandoned nooks.

"Shelby," he breathed as his thumb stroked the underside of her left breast, "I've never in my life seen a more stunning image than you naked in the moonlight."

His skin was smooth, not in a freshly waxed way. The man had little to no hair on his chest. There was no ink or scars marring the perfection that was his body, only a key on a dog tag chain, and she didn't feel worthy. Men as beautiful as him barely existed in the world, let alone noticed a woman like her.

As he pulled her to his chest, her rocking and his tiny thrusts up were stretching out the moment in a painfully sweet, sensational way, drawing out the orgasm for both her and him.

"I lied to you, Shelby," he whispered in her ear as his rhythm increased, and she had to struggle to hear his words as he rolled them both on their sides, angling himself as he pulled out nearly to the tip before gliding back into her. "I said I would fuck you until sunrise, but I didn't realize I could actually make love to a woman until I found you. It wasn't the length of time that I'd be in you, but the method."

"Daniel," she said, feeling the urgency in her own body to quicken the pace.

"It wasn't on purpose," he said apologetically, not letting her hips move faster than he wanted. "I've never felt a woman as perfect as you, and the moment I tasted you, my body shifted in a way I didn't know possible."

"What if I want a hard fuck?" she questioned, and his eyes devilishly glinted.

"Is that a question or a request?" His hand brushed her hair to the side. "Because there is little I wouldn't do for you."

"Then fuck me. You can worship my trembling body after you've sent me over the edge."

"I'm pretty sure I already did that." His smirk now matched his eyes as his pace began quickening. "Are you ready for hard, fast, and unrelenting?"

"Are you?" The challenge was empty to the man who slipped fully from her core.

The audible gasp from her annoyance and her body left on the edge was quickly replaced with a cry as he flipped her over and yanked her up onto her knees. A slap on her ass sent a sting across her skin as he angled himself behind her and pressed between her shoulder blades until her chest was on the blanket. Entering her, he had his fingers digging into her hips. He slammed inside her over and over as she clutched the blanket and knew in a moment her body was no longer hers. He controlled her pleasure, the heat rushing over her body, the skin that rose, and every tingle stinging and biting at her was because of him.

The rushing in her ears, the stars in her eyes, and the fact her knees were burning and she didn't give a good goddamn.

He was inside her, all around her, and found her stunning. Daniel's words were as strong as his actions, and when her body quivered around his length, he took two more strokes before draping over her and kissing along her spine as he emptied inside her.

His arms then snaked around the front of her, and they rolled to the side, spooning naked on the beach as the world came back into focus. The snap and crackle of the fire, the waves, and his lips laying butterfly kisses on her shoulders. She wasn't cold. How could she be, wrapped up in his arms?

The refreshing nature of a man unable to lie was like learning to ride a bike again after abandoning the mode of transportation for fifty years. Emotions and actions feel familiar, but you're sure that last time, leaning this way or that caused you to fall and scrape your leg. How wrong was it that honesty was the hardest thing to trust?

"How am I different?" she questioned as he trailed kisses from her neck, over her shoulders, and down to her elbow. The man was taking stock of her, memorizing each curve and inch of her body as he sat propped up on one arm. His free hand was occupied by floating over her belly with just the pads of his fingers as if he were reading braille that told him all about her.

"You tell me. Why aren't you judging me or calling me a fool? My crazy thoughts haven't scared you away."

Her hand reached back to cradle his face as she lightly kissed his lips. "I don't believe you've never had anyone who saw the truth of you behind the crazy."

"I don't think mothers count." He rolled onto his back, and she shifted to curl under his arm, their legs twining and his hand stroking along her spine. "Outside of Greek tragedies."

"There, right there, knowing about Oedipus, why do people think you're stupid?"

"Mostly because they don't believe I know what I'm talking about," he said flippantly as she began playing with his key. "You rarely have to say things twice to me. In Vegas they're used to it and know I'm not saying they're dumb when I correct them. Most think you're being flippant or disrespectful."

His hand slipped into hers, making her drop the key she'd been playing with, and he brushed his lips along her knuckles. Much like the first time it happened, she became weak. Thankfully she was not only lying down, but in his arms to boot. Her mind did what women's minds tended to do. He didn't want her touch, and every part of her mind needed to know why.

"That the key for your place in Vegas?"

"No." His tone was harsh and foreboding, a warning without malice.

They weren't in the place to discuss this. Shelby curled in tighter to him with the temperature cooling as the moon moved across the night sky. No matter the man, there was one part of riding a bike she knew. When to stop. He wrapped the blanket around their bodies, and soon they were moving into a slow lovemaking, the kind to allow your senses to fully invest in the moment instead of exploding and slowly coming down. This was the rise, the cresting the top of the hill before dipping down and coming back to the horizon. There was no him or her, and when both of them were at the moment of orgasm, they locked on and rode the wave together. Both trembled as their mouths fused for the last time before they began drifting into sleep, hands stroking along their sweat- and sand-covered bodies.

"Um, Shelby?" Fubar's nervous tone had her pausing from worry. "I think I know why there aren't people at this beach at night."

"Why is that?"

"That last wave covered my toes."

Jumping up with a start, she watched as her shirt was dragged out toward the Pacific, thankfully snagging on a rock. Their clothes had been strewn around the blanket, but only one thing had escaped the high tide rolling in, Fubar's coat. Like a gentleman, he chased after all he could find as the water rose around them. Even the broken path they'd taken down from the road had water lapping at the bottom step.

Shelby did her best to roll up the blanket while laughing at the vision of Fubar naked in the surf, diving to get her shoe that had floated at least five feet out.

"Leave it!" she cried, thinking how insane and gallant it was for him to rescue the bobbing footwear. Thank goodness for foam soles.

Covered only in the blanket, she moved back to the wall, standing on tiptoes as his fingers ran through his hair to flip it from his eyes and he trudged through the thigh-high water with an armful of clothes and shoes. One of his boots floated in front of her, and she reached for it, causing her to scream from the cold seawater splashing at her calves.

"Leave it," he joked as he finally made his way with most of their clothes, soaked, and he didn't have so much as a grimace on his face. Instead he shifted all the items to one hand and used the other to grab her by the back of the neck and kiss the ever-loving shit out of her. "You didn't run away."

"Why would I?"

"Because I pulled a me. I fucked up a beautiful situation."

They moved up the steps high enough they could wring out their clothing and do their best to wrestle themselves into it.

"You did have my clothes," she said, slapping her pants against the rocks in hopes of beating the water from them.

"You had a blanket."

"True, and how dare you not know the coastal tides better?"

"I should," he said, and there was a hint of him being scolded for being unprepared lingering in his eyes.

Cradling his face, she brought his lips to hers before saying, "These are the moments I cherish, you running out into the ocean naked to save my shoes. Not all fuckups are beyond repair. You know that, right?"

"You know the water is cold," he said as she glanced down only to find he'd successfully got his wet jeans on.

"Yeah, well, I have a place for you to warm up."

* * *

Shelby spending a whole day with Fubar had him playing the what-ifs and trying his best to discover a day in the Bay like no other. Only she'd grown up in the area, so wandering through redwoods or taking a trolley, being able to wander past the Painted Ladies or hang in a park, weren't exactly new experiences for her.

When he woke in her apartment, it was from a call, not the alarm. She was in the shower, so answering on speaker wasn't an issue.

"Speak."

"Is that any way to answer a phone?" Bo's gravelly voice bounced around the room. "Speak. What happened to *hello*?"

"I'm sorry, sir, hello. How can I help you?"

"I've got cars backed up waiting on you."

"Me?"

Fubar had been helping out being the lifter and eyes for the man as he recovered, but Shelby said her cousin Quinton had taken her spot. Assuming a male cousin would be enough for the shop had been an error on his part.

"Yes, you. Quinton can run the register, but he's the type that would put unleaded in a diesel."

"Well, let me finish getting dressed, and I'll be there in ten."

"Good, if Shelby gives you any trouble, tell her Pops made the call."

Swallowing back the unease of the man assuming his granddaughter was with him was the last bit of sobering he needed from the night before. Fubar snapped the phone closed right as Shelby came out with a few rivulets of water on her shoulder, wrapped in a fluffy beige towel tucked right above her breast.

"Everything okay?" she questioned.

"That depends. How mad do you get when plans have to change? I have a minute-by-minute agenda, but now I can't go."

"You want me to go by myself?"

"No," he said, glancing at his watch and doing the calculations needed for time to the shop. "But Bo called and expects me to be there today. I'd just been showing up because of you, but now he depends on me."

The sensation was new. For the most part he was a burden,

not a blessing. Most breathed a sigh of relief when he didn't show. He couldn't remember the last time someone called to see where he was, outside of club members needing him to do a task.

"He did say if you gave me any trouble—"

One hand went up to stop him, while the other covered her face. "He knows about us then?"

"I didn't confirm or deny where I was," he said.

"Well, I guess you have to go then." She dropped the towel to the floor and spun on the ball of her foot toward the closet.

Reaching out, he caught her arm and tugged her to him. Her damp form pressed into his as he kissed the back of her neck. "I told him ten minutes."

"But my apartment can't be more than four."

"Wonder what I could do in six minutes?"

One of the things Fubar needed to recognize was that having sex in a relationship meant upping his condom supply. Then again, monogamy could offer him a chance to ditch them altogether. A thought for another time. At this point he needed to get to Bo's.

Fubar made it with twenty seconds to spare and the taste of Shelby on his lips. For the first time, his running wasn't a bad thing. It had led him to where he belonged. It had been fast, but nowhere near as fast as Ice and Bree. He'd taken his time to move slowly with Shelby. Hell, he actually got to know more than her first name this time, and he'd been too distracted to put on a show for her. The woman got him. She understood the whats and hows of it all, at least so far, and his freak flag had flown pretty damn high around her.

She didn't know his past, but was quickly becoming his

future. One he'd make wherever she wanted. Vegas was just what he knew. There was no kinship to or affection for the city. His father bailing him out was a double-edged sword. Grasping the key on his necklace, he ran the useless piece of metal along the chain, the ticking setting him to rights a bit as he remembered the day it stopped working: when his father figured out his mother had let him have a copy so he could go in to wash his clothes and get food. Fubar had only done it a handful of times, but when he went to the door with his arm scraped to shit, there was a coded lock on the door. No longer could he get in without knowing the numbers, and there was no way his mother would take that chance. Not when his father would beat her, then change it.

She was soft on her children, he would say, while using a belt on Fubar, his brother, or her. Never his sister, but then again, he left before she hit double digits and got wild. Left well before what should have been his graduation because he couldn't see the look of failure glaring at him anymore for merely existing and being slightly different than the norm.

He parked his Harley and rushed toward the door, only to find it locked. All the bays were shut, and inside, not so much as the sound of a wrench turning.

"Hey, what gives?" a neighborhood kid that came through on his way to school asked.

Scanning the area for anything out of place, Fubar caught a chill when he saw Nevada plates parked next to the cars they should be working on right now.

"Nothing. Do me a favor. You know the Sin City club down the street?" he asked as he fumbled with his phone.

"My mom won't let me walk on that side of the street," the

kid said, his eyes wide and head shaking as he took off in the other direction.

Fuck. Part of him wanted to rush back to Shelby to make sure she was fine, but the other part knew the Brambillas had found him. The blowback of Shelby being with him had him reaching out to the clubhouse. No answer, of course, who the fuck would be there this time of the morning? His only hope was Toad being a gym rat.

"Sin Gym, how can I help you?"

"I need Toad, now."

"He's in the middle of a massive set. Can I take a message?"

"Are you fucking kidding me?" Fubar bit right as one of the Brambillas' men cocked a gun and pressed it to the back of his head.

"Be rude. Hang up without saying goodbye," the man with a bit of a Jersey accent stated, and Fubar clicked the phone shut. "And here we thought you were the stupid one of the Sinners."

"Common misconception. I'm pretty good at following orders," Fubar said.

"I got him. Open up the bay," the man said while shoving Fubar forward. The first garage door opened enough for him to walk in and see Tito, Marvin, Bo, and the man he assumed was Quinton gagged with their hands bound and tied to one of the lifts.

"Let the old man down if nothing else. What can he do? He's practically blind, and his bones might as well be kindling."

"Maybe we should put him out of his misery?" the head Brambilla said as he nodded to a henchman.

"You do, and I hate to say it, but the Griffins run Oakland."

It took every ounce of learning in Fubar to lie convincingly and not go too far. "This place look like it makes money? Hell, it barely makes sense. A blind mechanic runs the damn thing. It's a front for the Oak Ridge Boys. They run this part of the town, and I was sent in to try to build a bridge with the Sinners."

"Oak Ridge Boys, you say?" The big man pulled a cigarette pack from his shirt pocket and tapped one out. "I think I've heard of them. You hear of them, Jimmy?"

"Nah, but I don't keep up with the coloreds and what they do," the skinnier of the two men said, and Quinton shook his head, hopefully having gotten the country music reference. Then again, the blatant racism on full display may have been to blame.

"Yeah well, if this place doesn't open for business soon, people are going to start asking questions."

Fubar took in all the bound men. Bruising was evident. Bo's eyes narrowed from pain, and his fingernails were bluish white from lack of oxygen. The man needed to get down soon, or he might lose his damn hands. Circulation was bad enough in the elderly. He couldn't keep this up for too long. Who knew how long the man had been hanging there while Fubar had a quickie with Shelby. Quinton had a cut above his left eye quite a few layers deep and in need of stitches.

"It's funny that thing you said about asking questions. I have a woman asking me questions daily, making me have to do a little investigating into your club in Vegas," he said. "Vivian Mancinni."

"Never heard of her."

"What about Mario?" Jimmy spat.

"Brother named Luigi? Likes mushrooms?" That earned

Fubar a knock to the back of his head. By the weight of it, he was sure a gun was involved. Sadly, he could catalog hits and where they came from pretty easily. He had the experience, but what they didn't understand was he also had the rage.

A rage from them hurting people that had made him laugh, trusted him, listened, and took in the stranger knowing danger would probably follow. He should have left well enough alone after his bike was fixed, but he couldn't walk away from Shelby. At night she was his only thought, and when in her presence, his only desire.

Once again he'd fucked up, but it wasn't just his life he was destroying. It was the Griffins'. Of all he'd done wrong in life, this was the worst. He wished he could lose himself in the fog of violence, but too many factors were in the way. The kind of factors that tore at the heart he'd never thought he possessed.

"I heard you were a smart-ass," the Boss said. "Vivian's a religious sort, wants to bury her husband on consecrated ground."

"What does that have to do with me?"

"Heard you were the one who killed him," the Boss accused, and Fubar did his best to keep his mouth shut. His brothers wouldn't have told on him, but that didn't mean the man couldn't suss out the fact only one Sinner was no longer in town. "Didn't take long to find you. Seems you found the cops pretty quick here."

Inventory needed to be taken, and he knew where every potential weapon was, but they had one weapon he had never fought against—people he cared about beyond basic humanity, ones he may have to sacrifice his life to save.

eight

SHELBY GIGGLED at Fubar's list of activities for the day while nibbling on her thumbnail. It was a "best of both sides of the bay" tour. Going down Lombard Street so he could *"be the one screaming this time."* Eating at Jack London Square. Cable car rides, the Wharf, zoos, walks through the Fairyland, an edible garden, and more. There was no way anyone could get through them all and actually see them, but it was cute he had minute-by-minute ideas with a perfect loop going from her apartment and back through both cities. Who knows, maybe he'd cracked the code for days off.

Lord knows Sunday had been a very blessed day between the two of them. Praises to the Almighty were made, and it was nice to have time to really be with him without engines roaring or the ocean getting them wet. Though the wet ride back, while chilly, had been all she could have ever dreamed of, especially when he made sure no sand was on her body as they warmed up in the shower. Once she had given in to her desires, he took full advantage.

Part of her wanted to go to the places and take pictures to send to him. Not Lombard Street, that was for the two of them to experience, but the rest. After getting dressed, she made her way down to the garage where she kept her car, only to be met with blaring alarms. Owners of other vehicles hit were talking to each other, and a squad car had just pulled into the lot. Double-clicking her lock shut down the alarm on her car, and the last of the victims did the same as they came down in work clothes.

Not the way to start the day for them. She wanted to be mad, but part of her heart lightened. Fubar was at the shop, and she could clean out the glass quick, toss down a blanket just in case, and make her way over to have it replaced. Then she could find another day for the two of them to go explore the Bay. Having both made it clear they weren't going to start anything without an agreement about the future had him looking for a real job instead of just helping her pops.

A few more black-and-white squads showed up, and she was able to wrangle one of the cops so she could fill out her report for insurance and take off. They suspected kids, but they'd check the security cameras to be sure. At best a vandalism charge might be filed, and while annoying, her heart was racing for another reason.

On her way to the shop, Shelby made a quick phone call, only to get voicemail. "Damn it, Quinton, you better be with a customer."

The morning rush would be in full swing. Only when she turned down the street, the bays were closed and lights off. No one was out at the pumps or going in and out of the store. What the hell? A mix of confusion and irritation had her drumming her fingers on the steering wheel as she pulled into the station next to Fubar's bike.

Dusting herself off as she got out, sure there was glass on her somewhere, she stomped her shoes a few times and walked toward the door. A shiver ran up her spine as her belly tightened because this was all sorts of wrong going on. She couldn't see anyone in the convenience part of the shop. Telling herself it was because Q was being a fuckup, she quickly pulled her phone out, worrying her grandfather had taken ill. Why else would they not be in the store?

Her key turned in the lock, and she opened the door to find the security system wasn't armed. When she tried calling, once again she landed in voicemail. He would have come to get her if Pops was hurt. Every part of her knew something was wrong, and when a man in a suit came from the garage area with a smarmy smile and a wicked laugh, her racing heart seized

"Hey Boss, you were right. The little girl came running to her granddad," the man said.

"Fuck," Fubar said, shaking his head as she entered a nightmare. Pops, Q, Tito, and Marvin all strung up and gagged and a gun pointed to the back of Fubar's head. "Damn it, Shelby, I had a plan for you."

"What is going on?" She tried to turn, only to have the smarmy man shove her toward Fubar, who caught her before she crashed to the floor.

Violently she was ripped from his arms as a big man said, "No, we're not gonna have any of that, lovebirds. This is what we call leverage."

"Tie him up, Jimmy," the man in charge said. "We don't want him getting ideas."

One of the men with slicked-back hair began binding Fubar's hands as the other man kept his gun securely at Fubar's temple.

Plan for her? What did he mean? Obviously whatever was going on here wasn't planned, or was it? How was this a thing? Wasn't the world supposed to slow down when it was dangerous, not speed up?

The man who'd caught her dug his fingers into her upper arms. She could feel them bruising and tried to break free, but Fubar shook his head no as they lowered the chain used for engines just enough to catch the binding. She watched as he was lifted in the air, causing his tiptoes to brush the floors he'd wanted to paint. Then Jimmy used him as a heavy bag, probably the only way he got to hit a man, tied up and unable to defend himself. Each blow made her wince as Fubar did his best to not grunt or cry out in pain.

Was this the danger she'd been avoiding thinking about? She wasn't stupid. She knew bikers lived dangerous lives at times. The Sinners were far from removed, but she'd purposely avoided the clubhouse and the men, as if Fubar was a loner and not part of the club, some weekend rider, instead of accepting the man that he was. He never lied, but that didn't mean she ever asked the question she was supposed to.

"Now, what can we do with this pretty little thing while you think about Mario?" the man holding her asked.

All the men bristled. Those tied up tried to break free, but it was the shift in Fubar's eyes that made her the most worried,

MICHEL PRINCE

afraid she'd lose sight of the man she loved as a monster emerged.

Part of him disappeared. It wasn't so much faded, but checked out. The man staring at her right now was not the man who'd been joking with her this morning. The one who'd held her in his arms for four and a half minutes while he somehow brought her to orgasm, timed to perfection as always because it was what he needed to keep him steady.

Shelby felt tears filling her eyes, unsure if the man holding her and rubbing against her back with his manhood like a damn humping dog would make those she loved most watch as he violated her.

"Who's Mario?" she asked through chattering teeth. "And what plan did you have for me?"

"We didn't have a plan so much, sweetness," the man behind her said as she snarled.

"I wasn't asking you," she snapped. "Fubar, was this part of your plan?"

"You're supposed to be going to the cable cars."

Oh, that plan. In a split second, she'd forgotten all about the sweet day her hard-ass biker boyfriend had planned for her. The one with her seeing the city in a whole new way. Destroyed the moment she saw the smashed-out window of her car.

"It was you?" She narrowed her eyes at Jimmy. "You smashed out my window?"

"Yeah, it was me." Jimmy beamed giving Fubar two more hard jabs. "It's been a while since I had so much fun with a bat."

"As for Mario, he went to your man's club," the big man they called Boss said, "put a few bills in some G-strings, and then disappeared. Since this one took off, I'm pretty sure he knows where he is."

"Why don't you ask him?" she questioned. "You didn't need to tie up my family."

"He's got a smart mouth, and we found motivation is key with the hardheaded, slow ones."

Shelby wasn't sure if she was more scared of what he was saying or insulted for Fubar. Everyone always underestimated him, and he used it to his advantage. That didn't mean he could take out four armed men by himself. She had to help the only way she could.

"Who's Mario, Fubar? I'm asking, not them," she said, and he twitched. Swallowing her fear and disgust, she asked again. "Fubar, tell me."

"Ask me no questions, Shelby," he said as if it was painful to speak as he dangled in the air.

"We both know you can't lie," she countered, razor blades cutting along her throat. "Is Mario why you're here?"

"Yes." His response was clipped.

"See? All we needed was the right motivation," the Boss said.

"Let my grandfather go," she snarled. "He has nothing to do with this."

"Doesn't he? He gave this man a place to work, acted like he didn't have a filthy murdering biker working for him."

"Like your hands are clean," Fubar said, only to get a hard blow to his solar plexus, making him arch backward.

"Hard head makes a sore ass," the Boss said. "I remember you bein' a kid getting tossed around by your dad, the great Sean Coney. Made his bones taking down my enemies. You ever put two and two together? Remember coming to my spot? Probably not. Your brother did. He plays by the rules. The great prosecutor that avoids the Brambillas. But you didn't avoid us, did you, Daniel? The fuckup of all fuckups."

"Who is Mario?" Shelby asked again, not wanting to know how dark Fubar's family was. Not after she heard about his mother being smacked around and him being locked out forever. Everyone had a copy of Pops' house key. Kicked out of the family? That could never happen.

"I think he's the guy that was beating on one of the girls at the club." Fubar was starting to swing a bit, but no one seemed to notice, or if they did, it was assumed it was part of Jimmy using him as a piñata.

"What did you do?" she asked, trying to figure out if she could get away from the son of a bitch holding her.

"Heard one of our girls cry out, ran over, started pounding," Fubar said, then gave her a wink. "I have an issue once I get started."

"Is that so?" the Boss said. "Well, I've got a similar issue. Where's the body?"

"Was he made?" Fubar asked. "I did pay attention growing up. Only the made men get retribution. Guess it's like your benefits package."

Shelby held her breath, watching the increase in Fubar's speed and knowing he was up to something, but she couldn't figure out what. It wasn't like he was on a swing at the playground. Abs of steel or not, the man couldn't be—

Now the world slowed. Sure, the engine crane could hold a thousand pounds, but it also had wheels, ones that hadn't been fully locked down, and Fubar was able to get closer to the wall.

With a huge swing, his leg flailed out, knocking the smarmy grin from Jimmy's face. The grip of her molester loosened just enough she was able to stomp on his foot and wrench one arm free. Her fist balled, she punched down, hitting the stiffness behind his zipper and making him drop instantly. The Boss was backing up. He pulled his gun and shot off two rounds as Fubar's feet moved up the wall high enough he was practically horizontal. The move was insane as he twisted again in a way that locked him tighter on the hook of the crane, but he was close to a toolbox, and the height was perfect. Climbing on top of the heavy metal box, he was able to get his bindings off the hook, sending the crane flying across the floor. The Boss had to move to get out of the way, and in a Fubar "luck of the draw" way, one of the wheels hit a divot in the concrete, sending the equipment in a possessed way after him.

With the big man struggling to find breath, Jimmy knocked senseless, and the Boss working to toss heavy metal off his body, there was only one man left staring down Fubar, his gun pressing Pops' temple. Fubar crouched as he balanced on the top of the toolbox. She could see the calculations going off in his head, when the big man snagged her ankle, having recovered himself enough to fight back.

Her face planted on the hard floor, sending an eruption of pain across her skull, and a metallic taste filled her mouth. The mix of oil from the floor and blood spewing from her nose. Stars filled her eyes, and she tried to figure out what had happened, as she was being reeled in by her legs.

"Now I'm really going to have fun with you, bitch," he growled as every movement set off vertigo and the world spun out beneath her.

***

Triggered, with no chance of reprieve for the one who'd set it off, Fubar bounded from the top of the toolbox. It wasn't the gunshot from the Boss or the look on Bo's face right before he tackled the man holding a gun to his head. Fubar lost all control when he saw Shelby try to push up from the floor on her hands with blood flowing down her face. There weren't enough men in all of the Brambilla family to sate his anger.

The vacuum pulling him into a space of disassociation had him slamming the man's head over and over, until a bar cracked his back. Turning with hands still bound, he caught the bar as Jimmy's eyes widened. Caught in a game of tug-of-war, four hands on the steel tire iron, they danced. Fubar's muscles burned, and he hated that he couldn't adjust his grip. The look of fear staring back at him was a shot of adrenaline straight to his heart as he bent the man backward, angling him to the counter, as he moved the solid metal to the man's neck and pressed down. The resistance was minimal as the pale face turned bright red and he tried to cough out a concession that Fubar couldn't hear.

By the time the big dude came to help Jimmy, his eyes had rolled back and his fingers were uncurling. Fubar could feel the shift in air as he met him with a swing that had once been common in Candlestick Park. He knocked the man directly in the temple as his hand reached out, grasping for Fubar's neck—only for him to slump forward before dropping to the floor with a shot to the back of his head.

Glancing to the left, Fubar saw Shelby on her knees with the gun that had been being held to her grandfather's head in her hands. They were in this together, and while he may have knocked the man senseless, she was probably the one who killed him.

Spinning the tire iron in his hand like his father did with a nightstick, he walked methodically over to where the Boss had finally extricated himself from under the equipment. Shelby's hands shook with the barrel of the gun pointed at the Boss, he bobbed and weaved to make himself a moving target as Toad burst through from the store with Frenchie, Ace, Frankenstein, and Birdy in tow.

"What the fuck, man?" he said, but Fubar didn't dare break the gaze with the Boss.

It was the sound of five other guns being drawn that finally had the Boss release the handle of his nine millimeter and let it spin on his trigger finger. Every part of Fubar wanted to have the sanction to split the head of the man—who'd threatened not only him, but the family he'd created in barely a month in Oakland—open like a piñata. But there was something other than rage driving him for the first time since getting into a fight.

Worry. Worry over the woman who'd face-planted on the concrete, sending him into this space. Worry over Bo's hands and Quinton's cut on his forehead. Worry that he'd bring heat to the Oakland Chapter. Worry Shelby could be pulled into a murder and punished all because he lost it for a few minutes in Vegas. Worry over the fact she may never look at him the same way again, and the biggest worry of all, if she could get past this to be with him. Worry that the Brambillas would send more men next time.

"This is over." Fubar stepped to the Boss as Toad took his

gun and Frankenstein did a pat down of the man. "You hear me? I killed Mario, much like I'm sure I killed that piece of shit over there." He pointed to the man whose head was one with the concrete at this point. "I don't know where the fuck the man's body is because my Prez told me to go, so I did."

Fubar made his way to one of the tool chests and removed a box cutter to free himself from the bindings.

"Not sure what level you are with the Brambillas or what level these motherfuckers were, but it doesn't fucking matter. You came after mine, which means I'll put you somewhere at high tide so your ass will be in the middle of the ocean before they know you're gone."

Freed, he turned to get the rest of the men down, only to see Birdy had used a switchblade to get them loose already. It was Shelby that made him pause. Still on her knees, her dark curls framing her face as she stared at the floor, the gun held lightly in her hands, making his heart clench.

"Bodies don't come back," King said, having entered the room where the Boss was now seated on a rolling stool. The scraggly bearded head of the Oakland Sinners crouched a bit to be eye to eye with the Boss. "If Grimm gives you this Mario, you'll use the right funeral home for his service. Closed casket. He's been in the elements for over a month, not sure what might have gotten to him."

There was a Sinners dumping ground outside Vegas, in the desert. Much like there was probably one for the Brambilla, Bianchi, Carbon, and Mexicali groups. Gotta love bright open spaces where coyotes roam and people don't.

"I promised the widow his ring. That's all she wants," the Boss grumbled.

"That doesn't seem too hard of an ask." King stood and straightened. "But don't come to my city again with this bullshit. Because we've got our own guys I'm sure you didn't get permission from to be here."

With the club leadership dealing with the remaining Brambilla member, Fubar knelt in front of Shelby, her head downturned, as he removed a bandana from his pocket that he wore on long rides. The pale blue was quickly discolored with her blood as he dabbed it away from her nose and lip. She sat silent. Her lost was different than his. Her fight was as strong, though. He couldn't believe when she'd spoken up, trying to distract and get in the middle without so much as a tremble in her voice.

"I don't even know what to do now." Bo shook his head. "Forty years and the gunfire and violence stayed outside the doors. Is my grandbaby going to jail?"

"No," Fubar said emphatically, slipping the gun from her hand and passing it off to Toad for disposal. The man instantly removed the clip and dismantled the gun as if he was going to clean it.

"The police, we need—"

"We've got this, Bo." King placed a hand on the old man's shoulder and cut off his thoughts. "You head home. We'll get someone to take your grandson to the clinic to get stitches."

Quinton was sitting with a pissed-off look, as if he was about to tear into someone's ass, but there was a tinge of embarrassment for being tied up when the action happened. The man was going to go postal at some point over having bitch-like tendencies. That was a worry for another day.

Looking over his shoulder at Marvin and Tito, who were in a state of shock, Fubar asked, "You good?"

"Yeah, shit, this is nothing," Tito said, falling into the sarcasm most needed to survive trauma.

"What about Shelby?" Bo asked as he stopped by the door. "I can't leave my granddaughter."

"I'll bring her to your house," Fubar assured him. "You can both rest."

Scooping her up in his arms, he carried Shelby and placed her in the passenger side of her car. Toad came out to greet him before leaving.

"I'll come back and clean up my mess," Fubar offered.

"Shit, man, you earned your name today."

"You think she'll be okay? I mean, you guys have known her longer than me."

"Shelby shot the son of a bitch," Toad said with a shake of his head, "in an enclosed space. She probably just needs her hearing back."

"Hey Fubar," King said, approaching him and offering a hand. They clasped and pulled into each other, like a fucked-up hand wrestling match, and the man stared him down. "She yours? Claimed and shit?"

"That's what I'm planning."

"Good, so you're staying, transferring your patch?"

Fubar nodded. "If you'll have me. I have to say, I like the Cali life. Still got some places I need to check out."

"Get an apartment. The clubhouse is for crashing, not living," King ordered as more bikes began rolling into the parking lot along with a couple of vans. Yeah, they were going to do cleanup, and unlike the brother that he'd grown up with, these men were letting him care for his woman, not smacking him on the head and calling him a dipshit or asshole or fuckup.

The blanket she'd laid over the broken glass on the driver seat really didn't do the job, but at this point he needed to get her away from the Fill-Up and Fix-Up, broken window or not. He pulled out of the parking lot and headed toward Bo's home. The old man was walking, but when Fubar pulled to the curb to pick him up, he waved him off, so he continued until he pulled in front of the two-story home Shelby called her anchor.

Her head tilted a bit, and then she uncurled her fingers.

"That the key to Bo's?" he asked, and she shook her head no. He looked at the cuts and grooves of the silver key, marked a bit with scratches, and sat back to reach for the one no longer around his neck.

"It fell off," she said, "slid across the floor to my knee when—when he reached for you."

"I don't want it. It's a key to nowhere and a place that never really was."

She turned to him. The soft brown eyes he'd fallen so deeply in love with were coming back, not sparkling like they usually were, but back a bit from where she'd had to go to feel safe and protected.

"We were supposed to be going over the Golden Gate Bridge by now," she said. "Take me."

"But Bo?"

Her hand curled around his as she softly whispered "He'll be here when it's time to come home. My family will always be here for us."

nine

SIX MONTHS Later

"Hey, those tires aren't going to rotate themselves," Shelby barked at Tito and Fubar as they were jacking around thinking they were funny.

"Yes, boss lady," Tito said as the whir of the impact wrench to take off the lug nuts echoed in the garage.

"ADHD aside, Fubar, you can't let him distract you with shiny objects."

"What about you?" he said, wrapping his arms around her waist and pulling him to her. "Those *pretty brown eyes*."

"Breaking My Heart" by Mint Condition had been one of his favorites to play to get her dancing from the first line alone.

Something in Fubar had shifted when he tossed the old key from his house out of the window of her car in the middle of the Golden Gate Bridge. Traffic was backed up, and he had a good arm that sent the metal into the bay. Coming down had taken longer than the ride, and true to her word, Bo welcomed them in a few hours later. It was the space and time they both needed in the moment.

Her shock had come from the fear she felt for the first time around Fubar. Not of him, but that someone could beat him, take him from her, and she hadn't known a loss as great as that. Not her grandmother, or when her parents moved away. Not her job, or even a dog they had to put down when she was younger. This was deeper, more powerful, and the pain was nearly crippling. Part of her shock and zoning out came from the fact she feared he'd been taken already. When he carried her to the car, she was sure he was an angel and they'd both died.

"Quit it," she scolded. "You're supposed to be apprenticing."

"But I already know everything," he reminded her.

Between his prior experience and the fact the man could not only memorize books, but also comprehend them meant he did know his shit.

"That's not the point. You're a business owner. Set an example."

"Shelby," Bo called from the store with a coffee cup in his hand. "Customers don't want this junk."

"Not your problem anymore, Pops."

"Yes, it is. I'm the customer."

She gave Fubar a light kiss, and he held tighter. "Daniel, let me go."

"You know when you call me Daniel, letting go is the last thing I want to do."

"Shelby," Bo called again.

"Sir, are you loitering?" Fubar teased.

"Is there a ring on the finger of the girl you're holding on to? If not, let go," he bit back, and Shelby shook her head, pulling from Fubar to deal with her grandfather.

While Bo wasn't willing to sell the business outright, Fubar was in the process of buying the Fill-Up and Fix-Up. It would stay his even after Fubar fully owned it, but it was easier to get Fubar to change things in the place. First they painted the floor, but that was a bit more about covering up blood than aesthetics. The latest was destroying the old coffee machine and putting in a small one that made lattes and more. Her grandfather hated that he couldn't get a black coffee anymore. He could. He just thought it was too complicated. At least he was starting to step back as the cousins were coming around more to take him places. Most were already plotted out thanks to Fubar's list.

Now the business from the Sinners had increased, and she'd even been brave enough to join him at the clubhouse for parties. Sure, she was wearing a bit more leather now and riding bitch on Fubar's bike, but the biggest change in her life came from a man with the inability to lie to her who told her he loved her every day.

ace- by tamika brown

"WE'VE GOT A PROBLEM," T-Bone says, opening my office door without knocking. He's one of my brothers, a patched member of Sin City MC.

I stop flipping through the fucking paperwork sitting on my desk that I hate doing and wait for him to tell me the bullshit that's happening. I blew out a frustrated breath. I've told the guys so many times to fucking knock when the door is closed, especially when I'm doing paperwork because I have to concentrate.

If it's not a customer getting handsy with one of the girls on stage or my bartenders, somebody's trying to get over on us at the *Gameroom*. It's our gambling establishment in the back of my club, Sinful Desires. Typically, the Prospects manning the games can handle things on their own. I only step in when it's something serious.

"What the fuck is it now?" I growl.

Just once, I want things to go right in this place at night.

"It would be better if I just showed you."

T-Bone doesn't wait for me to respond and makes his way back the way he came. I stand and follow him out of my office and down the hall.

I briefly peek my head into the main showroom just to look things over. Chaos and Devil, two brothers who help out here, kept their eyes on the floor and bar.

T-Bone makes a left past the girls' dressing rooms and the bathrooms. Now I know it's some bullshit happening at the tables.

He presses his thumb to the reader, and the door opens with a push of pressurized air. Only Sinners can access the Gameroom and come and go as they please. I used the money from my trust fund to open one of the best damned establishments in Oakland. Everything I earn from this place goes to the club.

I step inside the room, and T-Bone closes the door behind us. The place is buzzing with excitement as loud music bumps through the speakers. I move deeper into the room to see Digger, a Prospect, has someone hemmed up in the corner while Slim, another Prospect, has a gun aimed at his head.

"What the hell is going on?"

I can clearly identify the man as Digger steps away from him.

"Ahh, shit." I run my hand through my hair. "What the fuck happened?"

This shit just threw my anxiety to another level. There's always something.

"This motherfucker thought he could cheat us by counting

fucking cards," Digger explains. "Then when Slim called him on it, he took a gotdamn swing at em'."

"You're fucking lying," the man spits back. "Do you know who the fuck I am?"

I do know who he is. Brantley Garfield. The All-Star catcher for the Oakland A's. He's a big motherfucker too, and the last thing we need is problems with him. If this got out, the media would be all over this shit, putting more eyes on my place. But there's no way in hell I can let this slide.

Always some shit.

"We do know who you are. And I don't give a fuck. You tried to cheat us out of our money. Do you have a fucking death wish or something?"

"I wasn't counting no cards," he implores.

I assumed the woman screaming his innocence is his date. I cut my eyes to her, and she shuts her trap; then I turn my attention back to the asshole before me.

He says he wasn't counting cards, but I know better. All of us do. He should be glad we don't fuck him up right here and now.

I move into his face. "Are you saying my guy here is lying?"

"I said I wasn't countin' no cards," the slight tremble in his voice reveals the fucker is lying, and he knows it too.

"Do you have a death wish, bitch?" I spit.

"I'm telling you the truth," he pleads on deaf ears.

He should really shut the hell up because he's pissing me off. Slim has yet to remove his gun from this son of a bitch's temple.

I face Digger. "Where's the money he won?"

"Still on the table," Digger answers.

"Get it," I say without turning away from Garfield.

Digger comes back and hands me a wad of cash. At first glance, there has to be more than five grand. Now, I'm no dummy. There's potential to win a shit load of money in our games, but not that much.

"Give me my fucking money!" Garfield growled.

I laugh. Hard.

"Your money? Motherfucker this is *our* money. Now get the fuck out of here before something happens to those knees you need to make those millions."

Garfield swallows so hard that his Adam's Apple bobs in his throat. It's a feat in itself, seeing how thick his neck is. Then his eyes hardened, and I could see his fingers twitching before he clenched them at his sides.

I smirk because he wants to buck. And I want him to. I'm itching to bust this fucker's kneecaps wide open. His eyes flick to the money, contemplating even with Slim's gun to his head.

My fists tighten at my sides. I'm ready for the motherfucker to get froggy. I have to admit, he's got guts if he thinks nothing will happen to him.

"Fuck this," I mutter, then punch him square in the ribs. Slim moves away as Garfield bowls over. Then I kick him in his left knee; the crack echoes within our circle. A hush settles over the crowd briefly before the murmurs start when he hits the floor in pain.

"Get him the fuck out of here!"

Digger grabs Garfield under one arm, and Slim grabs him under the other, dragging him out the back door with the sobbing woman trailing behind them.

"Fuck," I mumble and stuff the money in my pocket, heading out the door with T-Bone behind me.

"You gonna call King?" he asks as I head back to my office.

"Don't have any other choice, but I don't think Garfield will run his mouth. Not if he knows what's good for him."

"Of course, he won't," T-Bone chuckled. "Then he's got to explain being in a Sinners' establishment." T-Bone follows me to the door of my office.

"Take Chaos and do a round outside and in the parking lot. I want to make sure that fucker is gone."

"And if he's not?"

"Take out his other knee." I shrug, pushing the door open to my office then kicking it closed. It doesn't matter to me one way or the other if Garfield can play.

I slump in my office chair, then lean my head back, blowing out a cleansing breath before I have to explain to King why a fucking baseball All-Star now has a fucked-up knee, possibly two fucked up knees.

I pick up my cell to dial King's number. "On second thought, I think I'll just text him. I'm not in the mood to have this conversation."

Quickly, I type out what has happened and then let King know Brantley Garfield is banned from Sinful Desires.

Who the fuck is that?

I snort and shake my head because who the fuck doesn't know Brantley Garfield. Apparently, King.

Oakland A's starting catcher.

What happened?

Card counting. He won't be playing baseball for a while, either.

Shit. Is he going to be a problem?

It's a fair question. He's well-known in California, shit, perhaps across the nation, but I believe Garfield cares about his reputation, so he's not going to say shit.

Nah. I'm sure he doesn't want the media to know he was here at strip club stealing from one of the girls.

That's exactly what I will say to anyone who pokes their nose around Sinner's business. There's no need for anyone to know about the Gameroom.

As long as you take care of it, King adds.

It's handled.

I end the text. The shit load of paperwork on my desk is getting smaller. I need to finish it all before we close for the night and make sure the girls get home.

Then I need to be right back in the morning for a shipment of beer that's long overdue and conduct three interviews for a new bartender because the bartender quit for no damn reason. Well, other than he's a weak fuck. But the son of a bitch will be easy to replace. There's always someone looking for a job. In the meantime, Trick, one of the brothers who bartends on the side, agreed to man the bar until I find someone. I'm grateful, but that big motherfucker can't stay behind my bar for too long. He scares all my customers away, except for the ladies of course. And yes, we get plenty of ladies frequenting the place.

It's almost three in the morning. I just want to lay my ass down, but there's a knock at my office door just as I'm keying in the last of the numbers for the week. I key in the final digit and turn off my computer.

"Come in," I call out without looking up.

"The girls are gone," Devil informs me as he shuts the office door. "And we had to kick a trucker out for getting handsy with one of them."

I grunt in acknowledgement.

"Money from the tables tonight," he says, laying the moneybag on my desk.

I pinch the bridge of my nose. "I'm not counting that shit tonight."

"Doesn't matter to me," Devil says, shrugging.

"You all head out." I blow out a tired breath. "I'll lock it in the safe."

Devil nods and turns to leave.

One thing I can say about Devil is when he says it doesn't matter to him, it really doesn't. I hear the soft *click* of the door closing behind him.

I still have a few notes to jot down for my own records before I can call it a night. I glance at the clock, drop my pen on the desk then stretch.

It's been forty-five minutes since Devil dropped the money off. I'm so ready for this night to end. The pops and cracks of my joints are enough to tell me I can't do many more of these late nights.

I stand and swipe the money bag from my desk and make my way to the safe tucked away in a nook at the back of the room, then shut the door to the safe, allowing it to rearm itself.

What happened tonight with Garfield isn't normal for Sinners' establishments. Most people aren't stupid enough to try anything like he did. I try not to make a big deal of it and push it to the back of my mind.

"I'm getting too old for this shit," I mutter.

I'm forty-five, successful as hell and have to do my own

damned books. That's not sitting well with me. I've been thinking about bringing someone in to do the books. But for obvious reasons, there's a need to be careful who comes and goes from this place.

Finally, I push myself from my desk and head out of the office, flicking the lights off but leaving the hallway lights on from the girls' dressing room.

"You headed home or to the clubhouse?" Chaos asks, following me out of the front door.

"I told Devil you could leave."

Chaos grunts but doesn't say anything and continues to follow me out. I get it. We watch one another's backs, so I don't give him shit for waiting around even though I don't need it.

I lock the door and swap the keys in my pocket for my bike keys.

I smile as I walk towards my custom-painted Indian motorcycle. The chrome shines under the parking lot lights, highlighting the turquoise and cream paint. I love this fucking bike, and no one rides it but me. Hell, even the club whores I enjoy every now and again do not get to touch my shit.

I've had a few offers to buy it, but there's no way in hell I'd do that. I point them to Frenchie's Wild Road Indian motorcycle dealership if they want their own.

"I'm heading home." I throw my leg over the seat and settle behind the bars.

"See you at the clubhouse tomorrow, then," Chaos says, hopping on his own bike.

I turn the ignition, and my baby purrs. The rumble vibrates in my chest and calm falls over me. This is what it's all about, the roar of the engine and the wind blowing in my face and through my hair.

I give a two-finger salute to Chaos and slip my shades on as I pull out of my space and head to my house on the outskirts of town, away from the constant bustle of city life. For once, I'm proud to make my way to Jacobs Manor.

Buy you copy at Amazon

books by michel prince

Long Ranch Series

"Cowboys and love mixing it up."

One Last Rodeo-Novella

One Last Sunset ****

The Last to Know

The Last Laugh

At Long Last

Chrysalis Series

"The hardest part of growing up is learning you are worth more."

Chrysalis*

The Beam

Not Even Death

Unto Us

The Growing Strong Series

"Biology is the last thing that makes a family."

The Guardian's Heart**

The Queen's Heart

The Politician's Heart

The Teacher's Heart

The Frozen Series

"If your heart is frozen in time, can it still beat?"'

Shared Redemption

Redemption of Blood

Stolen Redemption

Love by the Yard Series

"Tackling love one down at a time."

First and Ten

Second and Short

Third and Long

Fourth and Goal

Encroachment

Steel MC Montana Charter Series

co-authored with Wren McCabe

"Steel sharpens Steel."

Roadkill

Lil' Mama

Preacher Girl

Lil' Bit

Free

Cream

Dreamer

Topaz

Nightingale

Doc

Turbo - ###

Steel MC- Origins Charter

co-authored with Wren McCabe

Encased by Steel

Cloaked by Steel- Coming Soon

Concealed by Steel- Coming Soon

Healed by Steel-Coming Soon

Permanent Hangover Series

Two Ink Minimum

Ink All Night

Mixed Ink

An Enchanted Bedtime Story
Fairytale Retellings

Stalked-Jack and the Beanstalk

A Need So Great-Rapunzel – Coming Soon

Aberration Series

The Amalgam #

The Shield

The Seer

The Soul Reader

RYD Series

At Her Service ##

Fully Covering Her

The Ojeda Chronicles

Amara Acquired

Love on the Run

Always a Groomsman

Sin City MC-Multi Author Series

Ice

Fubar

Stand-Alones

Silly Girl**

Unwrapping a Marriage-coauthored with Reana Malori*****

Mask of Fire

Kiss from a Rose

Triple B Baking Co-First Book in Hearts of Braden Series

Hollywood Lights, Austin Nights-Hell Yeah Kindle World

Muted Swan-A F'd Up Fairy Tale

By the Light of a Blizzard

Joyful Kitty

The Rotation

Love in the Land of Lakes- An anthology-Her Stranger

Festivals of Love-An Anthology-Tightly Wound

Beyond a Moment-Loving Hearts Anthology

*Winner 2014 Sweetest Romance IRAE

**Nominated for Book of the year 2013 LASR

***Nominated for a RONE 2014

**** Nominated for Best Contemporary IRAE 2015

***** Nominated for Summer Indie Book Award 2017

\# Finalist for MN Book of the Year 2022- YA

\#\# Finalist Imajinn Award 2022- Romance

5 Star Reader's Favorite Rank

\#\#\#-Finalist Heart Award 2023 from Oklahoma Romance Writer Guild

Coloring Book

Love in Every Shade

Stay up-to-date with the author, sign up for her newsletter:

Website:

www.MichelPrinceBooks.com

Facebook:

https://www.facebook.com/michel.prince.39?fref=ts

YouTube

https://tinyurl.com/yccqt593

about the author

USA Today Bestselling author, Michel Prince, graduated with a bachelor's degree in history and political science. Michel writes New Adult and adult contemporary, paranormal and Sci-fi romance as well as Young Adult adventure.

With characters yelling "It's my turn damn it!!!" She tries to explain to them that alas, she can only type a hundred and twenty words a minute and they will have to wait their turn. She knows they'll eventually find their way out of her head and to her fingertips and she looks forward to sharing them with you.

When Michel suppresses the voices in her head, she can be found cheering for her son in a variety of sports. She owes a huge thanks to her family for always being in her corner and especially her husband for supporting her every dream and never letting her give up.

Michel was awarded Elite Status with Rebel Ink Press in 2013, the service award for her local RWA chapter Midwest Fiction Writers in 2013 and 2014, and Sweetest Romance at IRAE 2015. In 2022 she was a finalist for Minnesota Book of the Year for Young Adult, a Finalist for Best Romance in the Imajinn and a 2023 Finalist for Heart Award.

She resides in the Twin Cities with her husband, son, and dogs, Bolt and Sawyer.

Made in the USA
Monee, IL
15 September 2023